**They were alone in the elevator, for probably less than a minute.**

But it felt a great deal longer. Catching her hand in his, he raised it to within an inch of his lips, his eyes suddenly dark and searching. When Stella gave a small nod, he planted a kiss on her fingers.

"Rob, I..." The doors were opening and they were back in a world where even at this hour, there would be someone around to see whatever passed between them.

And anything that did pass between them would be all about loss and regret. They'd changed each other's lives, and now everything was going to be focused on moving on.

"I know..."

Of course he did—he'd been there too. It was almost a relief not to have to put it into words because there was nothing that Stella could say that would reflect the way she felt.

Dear Reader,

You may already know that our wonderful editors choose the titles for our books—which I'm very grateful for as they always come up with something that's better than anything I can think of. But the title of this book *really* made me smile.

Rob and Stella are both surgeons; Stella works in London, while Rob has made a home in the Sussex countryside. And for a split second my reaction to the title of the book was "But Rob lives in the country..." Then I saw my obvious mistake. The "city surgeon" of this title is Stella. :)

And this is one of the things I really love about writing for Harlequin. Their strong and practical commitment to diversity and inclusion. The opportunity to confound all kinds of outdated expectations, including the one that women can't succeed in certain roles. How can stories about love be anything other than this?

I hope my book lives up to its gorgeous title and that you enjoy reading Rob and Stella's story!

*Annie* xx

# Country Fling with the City Surgeon

## ANNIE CLAYDON

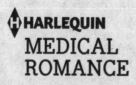

# HARLEQUIN®
## MEDICAL
## ROMANCE™

Recycling programs for this product may not exist in your area.

ISBN-13: 978-1-335-59545-4

Country Fling with the City Surgeon

Harlequin Enterprises ULC
22 Adelaide St. West, 41st Floor
Toronto, Ontario M5H 4E3, Canada
www.Harlequin.com

Printed in U.S.A.

Cursed with a poor sense of direction and a propensity to read, **Annie Claydon** spent much of her childhood lost in books. A degree in English literature followed by a career in computing didn't lead directly to her perfect job—writing romance for Harlequin—but she has no regrets in taking the scenic route. She lives in London, a city where getting lost can be a joy.

### Books by Annie Claydon

### Harlequin Medical Romance

*The Best Man and the Bridesmaid*
*Greek Island Fling to Forever*
*Falling for the Brooding Doc*
*The Doctor's Reunion to Remember*
*Risking It All for a Second Chance*
*From the Night Shift to Forever*
*Stranded with the Island Doctor*
*Snowbound by Her Off-Limits GP*
*Cinderella in the Surgeon's Castle*
*Children's Doc to Heal Her Heart*
*One Summer in Sydney*
*Healed by Her Rival Doc*

Visit the Author Profile page
at Harlequin.com for more titles.

**Praise for
Annie Claydon**

"A spellbinding contemporary medical romance
that will keep readers riveted to the page,
*Festive Fling with the Single Dad* is a highly
enjoyable treat from Annie Claydon's immensely
talented pen."

# CHAPTER ONE

'THIS IS JUST…lovely…' Stella Parry-Jones slowed her car, muttering to herself, before she gingerly turned into the dirt track ahead of her. There was nowhere to park on the narrow country road that led here, and it seemed that her car was going to have to take its chances with the wicked-looking thorns in the hedge to the left of the track.

But when she'd stopped at the village post office she'd been assured that this was the right way to go. And up ahead she could see a white painted house, nestling amongst a group of trees in the patchwork of fields. Since the first line of the address she'd been given was *The White House*, she'd take that as a sign she was going in the right direction.

*Physically* going in the right direction… Whether this was the right thing to be doing with a warm, clear Saturday morning was anyone's guess.

Going to see the man who'd had her job before her—that might be helpful or a big mistake. Asking for his help… Stella told herself that she had nothing to lose if Rob Franklin said *no*. She'd just drive back to London, tick this possibility off her list and she wouldn't have to think about it again.

If he said *yes,* then her patient potentially had a lot to gain.

She headed down the hill, towards the house. The wide gate that led into the driveway was open and she parked next to a battered SUV, which had clearly not managed to avoid the hedge on a couple of occasions. When she got out of her own vehicle to inspect for similar damage it was caked with grime, but Stella could at least congratulate herself on arriving here without having scratched her car.

The newly painted front door had no bell but there was a heavy brass knocker, fashioned in the shape of a dragon. Hoping that the dragon wasn't a warning, she grasped it firmly by its shiny snout and rapped loudly. No answer.

She'd been told that he would be here. Maybe *'in all day'* meant something different to Rob than it did to her and he expected her to wait if he was out. She'd met the previous Deputy Head of Reconstructive Surgery at the Thames Hospital in London only once, when he'd popped in to collect some paperwork from the HR department, and attend a hand-over meeting with Stella. The meeting had been awkward in the extreme, and Phil Chamberlain, the Head of Reconstructive Surgery, had been forced to do all of the talking, while Rob Franklin had tapped his foot, nodded and drunk tea.

Phil had drawn the meeting to a close quickly,

and on leaving the sum of her predecessor's advice to her had been a terse, *'Good luck with it, then.'*

Stella reminded herself that Rob Franklin had been going through a lot, back then. Phil had apologised to her, saying that he should never have allowed the meeting to go ahead because Rob was clearly having a bad day. Rob had been one of the brightest and the best, a brilliant surgeon and innovator and one of the best human beings that Phil knew, and his worried face as he ran for the lift to catch up with Rob and walk him out said more than all the rumours that had been flying around the department.

But three years was a long time. In the last year she'd seen Rob's name on several academic papers and been impressed with his clarity of thought and the bold simplicity of his solutions. When she'd floated the idea of contacting him with Phil, he'd agreed immediately and said that he would call Rob and find out if it was possible to set something up.

Stella knocked again. No answer. Phil wouldn't have let her come all this way if he'd thought there was any chance that Rob would duck out of their meeting, and Stella decided there must be a back door. She followed the paved path which ran around the house, past a well-tended kitchen garden.

A man was working in the dappled sunshine, amongst a cluster of fruit trees that lay beyond the garden. A gardener maybe, his tanned arms showed that he spent a lot of time outside. Stella opened her mouth to call out to him, but the words died in her throat.

Rob Franklin. Just the way that he moved, reaching to inspect the branches above his head, was different from when they'd last met. Since he wasn't looking her way, Stella could stare for a moment longer than she really needed to. He'd been wearing a suit when she'd seen him last, but she was sure that wouldn't have disguised these broad shoulders. And she would definitely have noticed the measured, relaxed grace with which he worked, clipping the extra fruit spurs so that those which remained would have more room to grow.

And then... It almost knocked Stella off her feet when he turned and, catching sight of her, he smiled. Taking a breath, to steady herself, she walked towards him.

'Stella?' It wasn't clear whether he recognised her or if first names were now just the way he worked. Still, the image of the man who'd looked straight through her and seemed to be waiting for any excuse to get out of the room was stronger than the one in front of her and she decided to play it safe.

'Yes. Mr Franklin?'

'No one calls me that any more. Rob, please. I'm hoping that your visit means that you've set aside my behaviour at our first meeting.'

He remembered. And he wasn't going to skirt around any awkward truths. That suited Stella. 'Of course. Rob.'

He nodded, bending to pick up the bag of clippings at his feet. 'You found your way all right?'

'Yes, I followed the directions that Phil gave me.' They *had* been accurate, even though they hadn't involved a postal address, which had prompted her satnav to claim that the place didn't exist. The smiling woman at the post office knew exactly where The White House was—about a mile along Snakes Lane. And it was indeed on the only road which ran west from Little Beddingford village.

He nodded, walking over to a large compost bin and emptying the bag of clippings. As he strode back towards her, pulling off his gardening gloves, she could see that his hands, at least, were still those of a surgeon, well-tended and clearly carefully protected. His eyes were grey-blue, but they seemed like a welcoming sky now, instead of freezing waters, and his face had lost that hollow-cheeked look that she remembered. Whether his smile was the same… Stella couldn't come to any conclusion on that, because Rob Franklin hadn't smiled once at their last meeting.

'Come inside. I dare say you could do with a cup of tea.'

Perhaps he was referring to the drive from London. Stella hoped so because she'd been working hard to conceal her surprise. Whatever. She could do with a drink, and the hospitality didn't seem out of character with Rob Franklin version two. Or maybe the man she'd first met was version two—everyone at work said that he'd changed in the six months before Stella had arrived—and the one she saw now was the real Rob Franklin. The way he'd been before stress had got the better of him and he'd burnt out.

Stella had quite deliberately not enquired too closely into what had happened. Her eyes were firmly fixed on success and whatever the pressures, whatever else she had to give up to make this job work, she wasn't going to go the way that Rob Franklin had. Although, right now, his complicated life trajectory didn't seem to have ended up so badly—he had a vague but unmistakable aura of relaxed happiness about him.

'How are things?' He threw the question over his shoulder as he made the tea. At least this was a question she could answer.

'Good. We've strengthened our links with several other reconstructive surgery units and that increased exchange of information is proving beneficial. We've also attracted a couple of newly qualified surgeons, who are showing a lot of potential…'

He turned suddenly. That smile again. It seemed that it was frequent enough now that Stella would have to start getting used to it.

'I was referring to you. Not so much the department.'

'That *is* how I'm doing. Right now, the department's the most important thing to me, and I don't have a lot of time for anything else.' Maybe she should make that clear. Because the thought had already occurred to her that this new Rob Franklin might make a fascinating dinner date, and if by any chance he thought the same of her she wouldn't have the self-control to say no.

He nodded, walking over to the kitchen table with two mugs of tea. 'Okay. Since that makes you happy, then perhaps we'd better get straight to it. What are you here for?'

No chatting about fruit trees. No walking out into the garden with their tea to take a tour of the vegetables. That was a relief, but suddenly it seemed that Stella had missed out on something as well.

'You're the best in the business, Rob.'

He shook his head slowly. 'I *was* the best in the business. Maybe.'

'I've read your papers.' Whatever he liked to say now, his work on developing suture techniques was still right at the cutting-edge. He must know that.

'That's theory. Unless you hadn't noticed, I don't practise any more. Not surgery, anyway.'

Stella resisted the temptation to ask what he was practising, because surgery was all she was interested in. 'We've used your work as a reference for our own surgical techniques, and in one of our training programmes. I believe you've consulted with equipment manufacturers...' She paused, waiting for his reaction.

That smile again. She was beginning to wish he wouldn't do that. 'Okay. Busted.'

'Then I can get on to what I want from you. If I may.'

'Be my guest.' He leaned back in his seat, propping one ankle onto the other knee. A picture of someone relaxed enough to listen and perfectly capable of saying no. Stella leaned down, taking her best shot at this out of her bag.

'This is a patient file, so...'

'Confidential. I understand.' He reached for the file and opened it. Stella had clipped the two pictures that she really wanted him to take notice of to the inside of the front cover. The shot of Anna's right profile showed a young woman with a good bone structure and a flawless complexion. Her left profile...

'Traffic accident?' Rob's expression had darkened suddenly.

'Yes. There were a number of bones broken and we're working on prosthetics to realign the shape of her face. Her left eye was saved, but as you can see there's a scar on her brow which has contracted, so it's pulling at her eyelid. There are problems with the way that her jaw has healed, which affect her bite and the overall shape of her face, and as you can see there's heavy scarring on her cheek and around her jaw.'

'Other injuries?' Rob rightly came to the conclusion that there must have been some reason why they'd waited so long to address this.

'Yes, she had internal injuries, which were operated on straight away. She's recovered very well from them, and we can think about further surgery now. As you know, there's a great deal that we can do for her, but it's going to take a lot of planning and skill. Anna's twenty-four years old, and she has a first-class law degree...'

Rob held up his hand. 'If you were about to paint a picture for me, that's not necessary. There's a lot we can fix...'

So he hadn't turned his back on surgery quite as completely as he claimed. Rob must have seen the involuntary quirk of her lips because he shot her a reproachful glance.

'There's a lot that *you* can fix. But you can't mend people's lives.'

'I've read your guidelines on what reconstructive surgery can and can't do.' Rob couldn't deny that he'd once been a surgeon, and the guidelines he'd written for the department were an excellent reminder on how to manage patients' expectations. 'But Anna's age is a factor when considering surgery, and her intended career is too, because her confidence in making someone's case in court has been undermined by her injuries. I was also going to mention that I've met her partner and that she's very supportive of Anna. You'll be well aware that family support's a factor too.'

'And her name's Anna.' Rob's gaze hadn't left the photographs, and he was clearly struggling to take a step back from the case.

'What else do you want me to call her? If you feel something when you look at these pictures, and you want to help, then maybe that's down to you.'

And maybe her reply was a little sharp. So what? Rob had opened the door on the discussion.

'I'd be interested in knowing exactly what you mean by the word *help.*'

It was a straight question that deserved a straight answer. And Rob must know that she'd come here with a shopping list.

She started to count on her fingers. 'I want to consult with someone with a detailed knowledge of skin grafting techniques, who isn't afraid of blending new techniques with tried and tested ones. Someone who can help plan and prioritise a complex set of surgical procedures. Someone with practical theatre expertise.'

'And you don't have all of those skills yourself?' Rob shot her an innocent look, as if this was actually a question that needed answering.

'I'm looking for someone who's as good as I am, in all of those areas. You know full well that discussion and collaboration make everyone better, and this is a complicated case so I feel it's going to be a vital part of the process.'

'Anything the matter with the guy in the office next to yours? Or did you just have a yen for some fresh air and a long car journey?' Rob's lips curved in half-smile, half-challenge that set Stella's pulse racing. He knew the answer to that question as well, but he was going to make her say it.

'Phil's job is to run the department. He advises, he puts people together when he believes they can form productive working relationships and he encourages collaboration. My job is to push boundaries, knowing that he has my back.'

'And you think I can push those boundaries with you?'

Stella was becoming a little impatient now. 'That's up to you to decide. I'll take whatever help you feel able to give me, in any of the areas I've outlined.'

Rob nodded thoughtfully. His frank manner had prompted frank responses, even though they barely knew each other. But that was good. Productive.

And…somehow intimate. The look in his grey-blue eyes made her shiver, and Stella needed to put aside the thought that she was becoming personally invested in getting Rob to agree to this. Nothing about it was personal, it was all business.

'Maybe I wish I could help and feel that I shouldn't.' He closed the file, putting it down on the kitchen table. There was something corrosive about the honesty in his eyes. Regret, over something that Stella couldn't see.

'May we talk about that?'

He seemed to be right on the edge of a *yes*. But then his phone rang and Rob apologised, taking the call. He listened for a moment, before briskly telling the person at the other end of the line that he'd *'deal with it'* and tucking his phone back into his pocket.

'I'm on call, and I have to make a visit.' He got to his feet. 'I'd like to answer your question, though, and I won't be any more than half an hour. Feel free to raid the fridge if you're hungry.'

'On call?' Stella raised an eyebrow. She was hungry, but she was a great deal more interested in what this sudden mission of Rob's was all about.

'Yes, I applied to retrain and I'm a junior doctor with the local GP's practice. I cover the village at weekends. It's not a very big place, as I'm sure you noticed during the minute and a half it took you to get from one end of the high street to the other, so I'm not called out all that often. This is just bad timing.'

'You're a *junior* doctor?' Today was turning out to be full of surprises.

He laughed suddenly. 'Yeah. Junior suits me at the moment, in lots of ways. You want to come along and try it out?'

That was an offer she couldn't refuse. 'Okay, yes, I'm interested. Who are we going to visit?'

'Emma Bradbury. Eighty years old, and lives alone. She's just been diagnosed with a heart condition and she's worried about her medication.'

# CHAPTER TWO

ROB HAD BEEN wondering about Phil's sudden emailed request for a meeting. They'd stayed in contact and spoke regularly on the phone, which was more to do with Phil's stubborn refusal to stop calling than any attempt on Rob's part to keep up with his London friends. He owed Phil big time, and that had a lot more to do with his agreement to meet Stella than anything else.

He couldn't recall her, but Phil's ill-concealed hint—*'You'll remember Stella, from the hand-over meeting'*—told him that they must have met and that she clearly remembered him. When he'd first caught sight of her, he'd realised just how far he'd come in the last three years.

The photograph on the hospital's website, which he'd consulted in preparation for her visit, was in black and white. She looked businesslike and sympathetic, which was clearly the aim of the shot. In real life, her red hair and green eyes were strikingly beautiful, and there was an honesty in her gaze that sent a tingle running down his spine. If he ever needed evidence of how messed-up he'd been when he'd left the Thames Hospital then he had it now because, however much he searched his memory, there was nothing pertaining to this fascinating, challenging woman.

It didn't help to think about the past. He'd struggled to make peace with it, and he'd come to a place where he could at least sleep at night and function during the day. Somehow, and without really considering that as one of his goals, he'd learned how to be happy.

Rob had made a lot of mistakes, let a lot of people down. Worst of all, he'd driven away the woman he'd promised to love with all his heart. He couldn't change any of that, but he could change what he did now. He'd taken one look at the photographs in the file that Stella had brought and the old excitement had taken hold. He could do something to help change Anna's life for the better…

Now he'd fallen into the trap of thinking of an anonymous patient by name. He was going to have to stop that, because getting involved opened up the possibility of further mistakes, more opportunities to let people down. Talking a few things through with Stella was an option—he was sure that she must have ideas on how best to treat her patient, and perhaps he could make a few suggestions. But there was no going back, and he had to keep this all at arm's length.

He went upstairs, quickly changing out of his gardening jeans and into a pair of chinos, which were quite respectable enough for work these days, even if they weren't quite as smart as Stella's dark blue summer dress. Picking up his medical bag from the cupboard under the stairs, he ushered her out of the front door. It was impossible to miss the look on her face as she breezed past him.

'If I wear a suit, Emma's going to think there's something really wrong with her. I don't want her to get the wrong idea.'

'And what about turning up with reinforcements?' Stella shot him a questioning look.

'I think we'll just say *friends,* shall we.' Rob thought better of the plan. 'Friends and colleagues.'

He opened the front passenger door of his car and she climbed in, leaving every nerve in his body suddenly on red alert at the subtle fragrance of her scent. As he walked around to the driver's door and started the car, he decided that, since he couldn't ignore the feeling, he had to just enjoy it and let it go.

'Anything I should know?' Stella reached for her seatbelt and the soft profile of her face prompted a sudden wave of longing.

'If she offers you cake, bear in mind that Emma makes the best coffee and walnut cake I've ever tasted.' Flippancy seemed to help with the *letting go* part of the process.

'It's good to know that this isn't a serious medical emergency.'

'It's serious. Just not an emergency yet.'

It was a seven-minute drive to Emma's cottage, and from the twitch of the net curtains she'd obviously been looking out for his car. She answered the door as soon as he pressed the bell, clearly having moved from her station behind the window to one behind the door.

'Thank you for coming, Rob. I hope I didn't interrupt anything.' Emma was looking at Stella, frank curiosity on her face.

'Rob and I were colleagues, when he used to work in London.' Stella spoke up before he got a chance to. 'I'm a doctor too, and I'm interested to see how his practice here compares with my own job. If you don't mind, that is…'

'Of course not, dear.' Emma stood back from the doorway, beckoning them both inside. 'Come and sit down. Do you have time for some tea?'

'If it's not too much trouble…' Stella smiled and Emma responded to her offer to help with the tea things by shepherding her through into the kitchen, leaving Rob to wait in the sitting room.

She was good with people. He heard the muffled sound of conversation floating through from the kitchen, and suddenly Emma laughed. She was still smiling as she led the way through into the sitting room, motioning to Stella to put the tray that she was carrying down on the table that stood in front of the sofa. It seemed that a three-minute acquaintance was enough for Stella to be allowed to pour the tea, while Emma insisted he tried a lemon drizzle cupcake.

'They're really good. I had a taste of one in the

kitchen…' Emma reacted to Stella's comment by offering her another cupcake, and Rob decided that they'd done quite enough bonding and it was time to get down to the medical details.

'What can I do for you, Emma?'

'It's my medication. I had my prescription delivered from the chemist this morning and I'm not sure whether it's right or not. I called them and they said it definitely was…' Emma frowned, the worried look returning to her face. 'I'm sorry to bother you on a Saturday, but you did tell me I had to take these tablets without fail, and I'm really not sure whether they've made a mistake or not.'

'That's fine, I'd far rather you called me if you have any concerns. Let's have a look at them.' Rob reached for the bag that was sitting next to the tea tray, opening it and studying its contents.

'What did the pharmacist say when you called?'

'Just that they'd sent me the right medicine and that I wasn't to worry. But they're not the same as the ones I had last time, these are called something different. Look.' Emma got to her feet, opening a drawer in the sideboard and taking out an empty packet.

'Yes, you're quite right. Many medicines have two names, a generic name and a brand name. The medicine they've sent you has exactly the same active ingredients, it just has a different package.'

Emma's face fell. 'I didn't know that. I'm sorry…'

'It's not your fault, Emma, they should have explained that to you. And they should be sending your medication a little earlier than this, so that you still have a few days' worth of the old ones, in case there are any mistakes or you have any queries. Since they did neither of those things, you were absolutely right in calling me to check.'

'That's good of you, Rob…' Emma was still looking a little sheepish.

'I wish more of my patients took the same notice as you do, Emma.' He glanced at Stella, and she nodded.

'Yes, some of mine could take a leaf out of your book. It's bound to worry you when you've been taking one drug and you get something that looks entirely different.'

Emma shrugged. 'I dare say they have my age on their records somewhere. They don't explain anything because they think I won't understand.'

'That's no excuse!' Stella's flash of outrage made Emma smile and Rob couldn't help following suit. Maybe the days when medicine made his heart race weren't quite as distant as he'd thought. And maybe he'd reached a place where he could deal with that.

'While I'm here, I'll just check your blood pressure and heart.' Rob reached into his bag and Emma shot him an enquiring look.

'Because you need to, or are you attempting to reassure me?'

He'd been expecting something of the sort. 'Don't you know me better than that?'

'Very well. If you'd needed to know what my blood pressure was, you would have already made an appointment with me. Since you never seem to like the word *attempt,* I'll accept your reassurances.' Emma smiled mischievously as she pulled up her sleeve and Rob wound the blood pressure cuff around her arm.

'Okay.' Rob checked the monitor. 'As expected, your blood pressure's fine and the same as it was the last time. You've been taking some gentle exercise and following the diet recommendations I gave you?'

'Yes. Do you want to see my notebook? I've been writing it all down.'

'It's okay, I trust you.' Rob turned his attention to the portable heart monitor and Emma held up her hand, ready for him to clip the sensor to her finger. Out of the corner of his eye, he saw Stella turn her gaze slightly towards the read-out, and Emma craned her neck to see it too.

He couldn't help feeling that there was an element of courtesy in the way that they both waited for his verdict; after all, they'd both seen enough of these to know what the reading meant without him telling them. Rob did his best to inject a suitable gravitas into his tone.

'That's fine. Steady as a rock. How's the reassurance coming along?'

'Very well. Thank you so much for coming, Rob.'

'It's my pleasure.' He packed up the monitors, putting them back into his bag and withdrawing the two books he'd brought with him. 'I finished the one you lent me, and I have one in return.'

'Oh! Splendid…' Emma took the books, glancing at the covers. 'I'm getting to really like these Scandinavian crime stories. They're quite different, aren't they?' Emma turned to Stella, who nodded. From the uncomprehending look in her eyes, it was clear that Stella wasn't a fan of murder mysteries. Probably not a fan of any kind of fiction— when Rob had had her job, he'd never had time for books. He'd only recently rediscovered the joy of reading for pleasure.

'I really liked the one you picked for me. The end came as quite a surprise.'

'Didn't see it coming, eh?' Emma got to her feet, examining the spines in the large bookcase in one corner of the room. 'Try this one for size.'

He took the book, stowing it away in his bag. Stella was persuaded to take some lemon drizzle cupcakes with her for later and they walked out into the sunshine, leaving Emma smiling at her front door.

'This is such a beautiful place,' Stella murmured as they drove through country lanes, back to the house.

'Yeah. I like living here.' He turned onto the dirt track, missing the hedge by mere inches. Maybe he needed to concentrate a little more on his driving, but Stella made that difficult.

When she got out of the car she hesitated, and then seemed to come to a decision. 'You're done with London, aren't you?'

The question surprised him. But when he thought about it, the answer had been there all the time. 'Yes, I am.'

'Is there anything more for us to say, then?'

This place had taken him in and nursed him back to health. More than that, it was somewhere he belonged. It would be easy to tell Stella that he'd never go back to London—that was *a* truth, if not the whole truth. He could allow her to believe that she'd done her best but that there was no shifting his resolve.

Or he could follow his instincts. Believe in the straightforward honesty between them, which seemed to have just clicked into place, without any particular effort on Rob's part. The thing about having a home, a solid base, was that it allowed him to reach out and explore whether what seemed impossible really was out of the question.

'Am I going to have to move house in order to consult with you?'

Stella smiled suddenly, and Rob knew that was what she wanted to hear. 'Absolutely not.'

'Then we have more to say.'

# CHAPTER THREE

MAYBE STELLA SHOULD remember what Phil had said to her on the way to the lift yesterday evening.

*'Don't walk away too quickly, Stella. Rob's a problem-solver and if he doesn't think he can help in the way you want him to, he'll try to work something out. He might even come up with a better solution...'*

She hadn't meant to issue Rob with an ultimatum. She'd simply meant to say that she realised now that his decision was more complicated than she'd thought. To acknowledge that asking for his help wasn't merely a matter of seeing whether he had space in his diary. He didn't just live here, he'd made an entirely different life for himself, and in the process he'd rejected the life that she had now.

The sun had moved in the sky and when they returned to Rob's kitchen light was streaming through the windows. He stowed his medical bag away under the stairs and started to go through the motions of making more tea. Stella didn't want any more tea and he probably didn't either, but it seemed to be Rob's way of giving himself time to think. He handed her a full mug, ignoring the file that still lay on the kitchen table and beckoning her outside.

They dawdled past the blackberry bushes at one end of the kitchen garden, and Rob stopped to snap off a withered shoot and throw it into the compost bin.

'We could go and see how your tomatoes are doing?' She gestured towards the ripening plants in the greenhouse. 'Or you could just tell me what I'm still doing here...'

Rob grinned suddenly. 'You're very frank.'

And she was still coming to grips with why that seemed so natural with Rob. 'It must be the country air. What's your excuse?'

'Not sure that I have one.' He began to stroll down towards the apple trees. 'Do you know why I left the Thames Hospital?'

'I don't know the details. I do know that it was a waste of a very good surgeon...'

He turned, blue steel flashing in his eyes. 'A waste? That's what you think my life is?'

'I'm sorry. I shouldn't have said that. I don't know the whole story and even if I did it's not my place to make value judgements.' She was doing it all the same. Wondering how he could reconcile throwing away all of that training and hard work, all of the dedication and expertise.

Rob pursed his lips and the thought occurred to Stella that maybe he couldn't reconcile it as well as he liked to make out. But it seemed that her apology had been accepted, and when he spoke his tone was matter-of-fact, as if he was trying to distance himself from the words.

'I thought that I could have it all. A great career, maybe some travel, a beautiful home and a family. For a while that didn't seem so difficult. My wife and I had a nice flat in London and we'd bought this place, reckoning on doing it up for weekends and holidays. I made deputy head of the department at thirty-four...' He turned towards her, the obvious question flashing in his eyes.

'Thirty-three.' Stella couldn't help rising to the bait.

He chuckled. 'I'm not going to hold that against you. How's it going?'

'It's good. I know I can't have it all. I don't have a partner or children, and I haven't got any big property development plans. But I have the one thing that I really want.'

He nodded. 'Maybe that's the answer, then. I didn't see it at the time, and I was always rushing, trying to push forward on too many different fronts. There were speaking engagements, even some talk of a possible publishing deal. Kate and I both liked to travel and we carved out some time for a few great holidays, but even then there was a lot to fit in and not much time to just sit in the sun and watch the world go by.'

Stella puffed out a breath. 'That's a lot for anyone to take on.'

'I'm not exactly idle now.' He sat down on a
bench in the shade of an old oak tree that stood
at the perimeter of the orchard. The scent of blos-
som and early summer growth hung light in the
air and Stella sat down next to him, stretching her
legs out in front of her.

She saw what he *hadn't* been saying, now. Anyone might feel a sense of failure if they'd left all
that behind, and perhaps there was an element of
trying to convince them both that the life he had
now was just as rewarding, but in different ways.

'Working as a GP and publishing your research,
you mean? And you've obviously done a lot here.'
The outside of the house looked freshly painted,
and the kitchen was obviously new.

He chuckled. 'Yeah. Sometimes I don't notice.'

He noticed. Stella didn't spend a lot of time on
her surroundings, they were either practical or
not practical as far as she was concerned, but this
place was a carefully constructed home. Maybe
Rob thought that it was a second best, something
he made do with because he'd lost what he really
wanted, and he expected her to judge him in the
same way. That wasn't what she'd come here to do.

'It looks as if you'll get apples from some of
those trees over there.' She waved her finger towards the group of larger trees that he'd been prun-
ing when she'd arrived.

Rob snorted with laughter. 'Yeah, okay. Don't

try to pretend that you know what you're talking about. I will get some fruit, but they're pear trees.'

'Very well pruned pear trees. I'm a surgeon and I notice those things, at least!' she shot back at him, grinning. Their frank exchanges about work spilled over all too easily into the personal, and that was surprisingly delicious.

'Thank you. I'm going to take that as a compliment.' He drained his cup, setting it down on the bench beside him. 'The trouble with building a house of cards is that you remove one and it all comes crashing down. My wife, Kate, left me, which was one of the best decisions she ever made. I took on too much, and in trying to keep everything going I forgot that marriage takes time and attention too. I knew that I'd failed her, and I moved out of the flat and got a bedsit near to the hospital and spent every waking moment there. Then I started to fail at my job.'

Stella stared at him, questions bubbling in her head. Rob must know what those questions were…

'It would have been very serious if that had affected a patient.' The knowing look in his eyes told her he understood what was making her heart thump uncomfortably in her chest. 'I couldn't sleep and I was getting stress headaches. I spoke to Phil about it, and we agreed I'd take a step back from surgery for a while, and concentrate on research and staff development. But a surgeon who doesn't trust himself to operate…'

Was a failure. Stella could see what Rob was thinking, even if he couldn't say it. 'Needs some help, through a really difficult time in his life?'

Rob shrugged. 'Whatever. My initial solution was that if I ignored it all, it might go away. That clearly wasn't the right one. I found myself working even harder and getting more stressed. Then I had a psychogenic seizure.'

'I'm sorry to hear that happened to you.' Stella tried to conceal her shock; psychogenic seizures were often mistaken for epileptic seizures at first, with the same shaking, jerking and loss of consciousness, but were actually often caused by serious psychological stress.

He nodded an acknowledgement. 'It lasted for fifteen minutes. I hit the floor of my office, conscious but unable to move or stop my limbs from shaking. By the time I was able to get up again I'd already thought through every possible medical option, and none of them were good.'

Rob was sticking to the facts, but it must have been terrifying. And suddenly that frank connection between them broke, a casualty of all the things he wasn't saying.

'You were at work?'

'Yeah. In case you're wondering how I managed to get fifteen uninterrupted minutes alone during the day, I was working late.'

Stella forced a smile in response, although Rob probably knew that the joke wasn't funny. 'That explains it. Of course, seizures *can* be a result of stress…'

Rob shot her a reproachful look. 'Were you asleep when they covered that at medical school? Never assume a seizure is caused by stress unless you've checked for everything else first.'

'But you said it was psychogenic—so you *did* go and get yourself checked out.'

'Yeah. I went to a friend of mine, who runs a private clinic. They ruled out all the usual suspects—heart problems, epilepsy, substance abuse—and while the results of all the tests were coming back it happened again. The day after I was diagnosed with stress and clinical depression, I put my resignation in at the hospital.'

'But…they're recognised medical conditions, with understood treatment paths. Did you think of taking sick leave?'

She saw his lip begin to curl, and then he shook his head. 'At the time, I would have seen that as a final expression of failure. I felt that I'd lost everything, and I needed to get away and start again. I'd insisted that Kate took our London flat in the divorce settlement, reckoning that was the least I could do, and we'd kept the house because neither of us were quite sure what to do with it. I bought out her share and came down here, more as a matter of getting away from the scene of the crime than anything.'

Stella turned the corners of her mouth down.

Failure wasn't a crime. Her father had often told her that pushing at the limits was all about finding out what was and wasn't possible. Why else would she have got into her car and driven down here this morning, on a mission that might well have failed?

'Would it be too much to expect that you took the usual route of counselling and medication?' Stella had a feeling that Rob had applied his own solutions to the difficulties he faced.

'Afraid so. I turned down the counselling that I was offered, and I didn't give the medication much of a chance either. As a doctor, it's not what I'd advise anyone else to do, but a complete change of scenery, somewhere I could start again and rebuild, was what worked for me. I've reached a place where I'm at peace with myself now, and I haven't had a seizure since I left London.'

'I didn't realise what I was asking of you, when I came down here. It's not that you don't want to help, is it?'

Rob shrugged. 'You didn't need to show me those photographs or tell me your patient's name. I know full well what's happened to her and what it must mean and I'd be there like a shot if I felt that there was something I could do. My hesitation is because I'm not sure that I'm the one who can help Anna.'

Should she take him at his word? Fail gracefully in her mission to gain his assistance in a way that preserved everything she already had, as her father had taught her? The feelings that Rob had awakened were just chemistry, and if the catalyst of their possible work together was removed, they'd fade quickly enough.

But she could feel that he was looking for a way to make this work. She was too. And if it *did* work then the benefits for Anna couldn't be ignored.

'Phil doesn't appear to think so.'

He let out a brusque laugh. 'I wondered when you were going to play that card…'

'I'm not playing a card, Rob. If you were entirely sure that there was nothing of any value you could add to Anna's treatment, we wouldn't be having this conversation, I'd be on my way back to London right now.' She thought she saw a slight downward quirk of his lips at the idea, and ignored it.

'I can see how coming back to work at the hospital is a big step, but we can keep things flexible. And the level of your involvement is entirely up to you, ranging from an informal consultative relationship to possible participation in Anna's surgery. If you can't do any of that, then I understand completely and there's no more to be said. But I'm really hoping that you want to keep talking and exploring possibilities.'

Simple. It made her position clear and left Rob the option of giving her a straight answer, so that they both knew where they stood. Why did that make her feel so breathless, all of a sudden?

'Okay, boss. How does here and now suit you? To explore possibilities.' The smile that hovered around his lips and the look in his eyes really weren't helping. They belonged in the realms of a delicious agreement between a man and a woman, and not a clearly thought through arrangement between two medical professionals.

Maybe Rob recognised that too, because his expression became suddenly thoughtful. That was only slightly less stirring than his smile, but Stella could deal with that if they both knew exactly what footing their relationship should be on.

'Here and now is fine with me. I don't have to be back in London at any particular time. My only condition is that you don't call me *boss*.' Rob clearly didn't have any intention of taking instructions from her in the foreseeable future.

He chuckled. 'As you wish. Any objections to lunch?'

Rob decided that a working lunch would be good. Not too much time for pleasantries, or getting to know each other too much. Despite his sudden wish to get to know Stella very well, it wasn't what he needed right now.

A ploughman's lunch, with salad and ginger beer, took only ten minutes to prepare, and relied on locally sourced ingredients to make it tasty. Stella followed him through to his office, which was when the plan of keeping this professional crumbled a little.

'Rob! You work here?' Stella was looking around her with the same expression of delight that he'd felt when his first spring here had provided the warmth for him to sit in the old orchid house, built on the side of the property, and he'd realised what it might become.

'Yep.'

Stella was looking up at the butterflies which had been disturbed by their entrance, and he couldn't help re-seeing the quiet magic through her eyes. The glazed partition which separated the conservatory area from his office space was folded back, and Stella nudged the door that led out into the garden closed.

'They'll all escape…' She grinned up at him.

'That's okay, they're not prisoners, and they escape all the time.' He nodded up towards the open vents in the glass ceiling. 'They come back again; the plants attract them. I keep the door to the house closed in the summer, so that they don't get through there.'

'You built this?'

'Renovated it. The previous owner grew orchids, but the windows were falling apart from lack of maintenance and so I had to replace them.' He put the tray that held their plates and glasses down on the desk, which together with a long work surface occupied a shaded area of his office. 'It was a big job, and I didn't get it finished until last year.'

'Doesn't it get really cold in the winter?'

'No, orchids need to be warm all year round, so it's built to keep the heat in. The back wall is attached to the house, and the side walls are both double thickness brickwork.' He gestured towards the fully glazed roof and front wall. 'This is all modern and well insulated. In fact, the main difficulty is keeping the place cool in the summertime.'

Stella nodded, gazing up at the two large fans that turned lazily over their heads, providing a comfortably cool breeze around the towering plants and shaded benches. Then another movement caught her eye. Sophie, the elderly labrador, generally spent the first couple of hours of her morning with Rob and then retreated to the peace and quiet of the conservatory to sleep, ignoring any comings and goings in the house. But she was awake and taking an interest now, and had quitted her dog basket to amble over towards them.

'Oh! You have a dog?' Stella bent down, holding out her hand and Sophie nuzzled against it.

'Sophie was a hearing dog. Her owner was an eighty-two-year-old man in very poor health and when he died his family weren't able to take Sophie. It looked as if she'd have to be put down.'

'So you gave her a home.' Stella smiled up at him. She and Sophie had clearly hit it off and

Sophie was leaning against Stella, almost knocking her off-balance.

'Hey, Soph. That's enough…' He tried to guide Sophie away, but Stella glared at him as she crouched down to Sophie's height, winding her arms around the dog's neck defiantly. 'It wasn't really a decision. She didn't have anywhere else to go, so she came with me.'

'And she's putting her paws up, now that she's retired?'

'Yeah, she's nearly fourteen now. She wakes up early, has something to eat and then she and I go for a walk down to the fruit trees and back again. That's about her limit for the morning and she comes in here for some peace and quiet. Although she still sometimes gives me a nudge when the post drops through the letterbox, just for old times' sake.'

'Anyone else live here that I might need to know about?' Stella squinted at the plants in the conservatory, obviously wondering what they might conceal.

'Not as far as I'm aware. There were a pair of robins nesting in the rafters this spring, but they've gone now.'

'Hmm.' Stella got to her feet. 'Those baby birds making a racket must have been awful when you were trying to concentrate.' She shot him an amused look.

'Dreadful. We were both glad when they were

gone, eh, Soph?' Rob opened his desk drawer and
Sophie ambled over to him, knowing that he was
about to produce the packet of dog treats. He saw
the look in Stella's eyes and couldn't resist handing
them over to her, so that she could make a fuss of
the dog. It seemed slightly at odds with the businesslike efficiency she'd displayed earlier on.

'I can see how this place would help anyone re-
gain their balance.'

'Not in the way you might be thinking. When
I first came here to live, I just wanted to get away
and didn't think too much about creature com-
forts. It was just before Christmas, and that was
a cold winter...'

She turned her gaze on him suddenly. Stella had
the knack of making a person want to talk, even
if she'd asked no specific question. He was falling hook, line and sinker for it, and he didn't even
*want* to put up a struggle.

'I remember.'

'Sitting things out until the summer wasn't an
option. It was freezing, none of the doors closed
properly, and you could feel the wind when you
stood within a couple of feet of the windows, so
I started to work on the place just to keep warm.
Then there was a heavy fall of snow at the end of
January, and I went out to help clear it in the village. That was when I first got to know Emma—
she runs a scheme to help with shopping when the
weather's bad, and she tapped me on the shoulder

and told me that I seemed to be making good head-way with the pavements and she could do with an-other volunteer. It wasn't really a question, more a demand.'

'She seems a resourceful woman.'

'You have no idea.' Maybe Stella did have some idea. She struck Rob as being a force to be reck-oned with too. 'The thing is that it wasn't the peace and quiet of the countryside that pulled me out of the ever-decreasing circles I'd found myself caught up in. It was a set of simple challenges, which had straightforward answers.'

'You haven't talked about this before, have you?'

Along with all of her other talents, Stella was perceptive and she read between the lines. Now suddenly seemed a very good time to back off and get things on a more professional footing, before Stella asked why he was talking about it now.

'Why don't we take another look at Anna's file?'

Stella paused, just long enough to let him know that she'd noticed the abrupt change of subject. Then she let him off the hook with a sudden smile and a quick shake of her head, in a *no matter* ges-ture that sent threads of golden light cascading through her beautiful hair. 'Thanks. I really ap-preciate it.'

Rob was beginning to feel a little less off-balance. A little less caught between the lure of returning to the one thing he'd really excelled at and his doubts about ever going back. What had happened three years ago had suddenly become very relevant to the decisions he made today, but as he and Stella worked through the file it felt as if today, and what they might do with it, was what really mattered.

'You're very thorough,' she murmured, looking at the practice suture kit that he'd taken from the cupboard, to assess the practicalities of one of the techniques they'd been discussing.

'And...?'

'You've kept yourself up-to-date with the latest techniques. You write papers. I don't suppose you have anything else up your sleeve?'

'Like what?'

Stella shrugged. 'Teaching, maybe?'

'I've thought about it. I've thought about a lot of things...' He leaned back in his seat, aware that Stella was watching him.

'I've come too far to go back now, Stella. I can only go forward. But maybe going forward includes working with you and using the skills I have to help Anna.'

He heard her catch her breath. When he looked up at her, Stella was trying to conceal a look of triumph.

'You're sure that's the right thing for you?' She had the grace to question his decision.

'No, but if it's a mistake then I dare say I'll learn something from it. And I want to make it clear that I *am* moving forward and that it'll be on my own terms.'

She allowed herself a smile. 'Mine too?'

Rob was suddenly aware of how close they were sitting. Up until now, it had just been a matter of sitting at the same desk, discussing the same things. Now it felt as if he needed to be breathing the same air as Stella if his own lungs were to work properly.

'That goes without saying, doesn't it?'

She leaned forward slightly. 'Say it anyway.'

So close. With two minds working together in such exact synchronicity, what could their bodies do…? Rob dismissed the thought quickly.

'On your terms too.' Why did that feel as if he'd just given himself to her? It was an obvious and productive grounding for any business relationship.

'Do we have a deal, then?' Stella held out her hand, looking him straight in the eye. A bargain was never really a bargain unless you looked a person in the eye, and Rob took her hand, feeling the pressure of her fingers around his. He'd expected her touch to be firm although not quite so soft, and the combination was making his blood boil.

'Yeah. We have a deal.' He let go of her hand before the heat between them became unbearable. 'Since you have what you came for, are you going to be on your way now? Or can you stay for dinner?'

She was thinking about it. And the way she

turned the corners of her mouth down told him that a few unnecessary hours spent having dinner together appealed to her. In someone who displayed the level of focus that Stella did, that was a small and very satisfying miracle.

'I shouldn't really. It looks as if it's about to rain, and it'll be dark soon. I wouldn't much fancy my chances on the lane leading back up to the road...' Stella looked up as a few drops of rain splashed onto the glazed roof, as if the weather was adding its own warning to her reservations.

'You could always stay over...'

Rob bit his tongue. It was a more natural offer when you lived in an out-of-the-way place, but perhaps his wish to get to know Stella better had something to do with it too. He was sure that there was some straightforward way of saying that his suggestion was a simple matter of practicality and not a come-on...

'The spare room's pretty well stocked with anything you might need. My sister makes sure of that—she often stays when she comes to visit.' That would have to do. He'd at least managed to incorporate the keywords *spare room* and *sister*.

And it seemed that Stella had got the message. She nodded, smiling.

'Thanks for the offer. Can we take a rain check and have dinner some time when you're down in London?'

So dinner was okay and staying over was to be

avoided. Now that he thought about it, that was a good decision. Friends, but not too close.

'I'd like that. I'll give Phil a call and set up a date for me to come up for a meeting, shall I?'

'Yes, that would be great.' Stella hesitated gratifyingly before she got to her feet. One more moment, surrounded by her scent. A small acknowledgement that she knew what had passed between them, and that this was more than just a professional connection.

And she was fighting it too. Rob was pretty clear about why he felt it would be a bad idea to take things any further than a professional friendship with Stella. The guilt of tearing everything down once was bad enough, and twice would be impossible to bear. It was less obvious why someone like Stella should feel that she had to exclude everything else but work from her life.

But it was too late to think about that now. Rob watched as she gathered her things together, putting Anna's file back into her bag. He'd put himself on a road that had no clear destination today, but Rob knew that he was committed now and couldn't retrace his steps.

# CHAPTER FOUR

WHEN SHE ARRIVED at work on Monday morning, Stella was still smarting slightly from the realisation that a perfectly innocent offer of dinner and Rob's spare room for the night had taken on an unintended secondary meaning in her head. She had to get this relationship onto a purely business footing and keep it there. But there was still a forbidden thrill of excitement when Phil called her into his office to tell her that he'd just spoken with Rob on the phone, and they'd arranged a meeting for two o'clock on Friday.

'There's one thing I'd like to make clear to you, Stella. You're the boss in this relationship.'

Stella shifted uncomfortably in her seat, wishing that Phil hadn't chosen to call it a *relationship*, even if he was only referring to a collaboration at work. 'I did tell him that he wasn't to call me *boss*.'

Phil chuckled. 'I'm glad he understands who's boss, even if you don't. And now that we're considering Rob's return...' Phil had an air of someone who was choosing his words carefully. 'Don't get me wrong, I think you made a very good decision in suggesting we ask Rob back and I'm personally delighted that he's open to working with us again. But you shouldn't let him have everything his own way.'

Stella thought for a moment. 'I've promised to be flexible, though. I think that's the right thing to do, in the circumstances, isn't it?'

'There's nothing wrong with flexibility and I completely agree with your approach. Rob's brilliant, one of the best surgeons I've ever seen, and he thinks outside the box. But he can be uncompromising at times…' Phil paused, clearly choosing his words carefully.

This conversation would be much easier if she just came clean. 'When Rob and I talked on Saturday, he told me that he'd been diagnosed with clinical depression and that he had several physical symptoms of stress when he left his job here.'

Phil nodded. 'I'm glad you had that conversation. You understand that it wouldn't have been appropriate for me to mention it if Rob hadn't done so himself.' Phil was always meticulous in protecting the confidentiality of all his staff, and everyone here appreciated that.

'Of course.'

'But now that you *do* know… He may have mentioned that I've been keeping in touch with him and I'm confident that he's fully recovered now. But he's been through a lot and my belief is that he needs a strong framework to support him while he's finding his feet.'

Stella nodded. Phil seemed to be overestimating

the amount of support that Rob would need, but he knew Rob a lot better than she did.

'I can provide the framework on one level, but I'm going to need you to back it up on a day-to-day basis, Stella.'

Maybe that was what Rob had meant when he'd called her *boss*. He wanted Stella to help him, and she'd turned him down without even stopping to think.

'I can do that, Phil. I'm committed to making this work.' Not just for Anna's sake, although she was the most important person in all of this. For Rob's sake, and maybe even for hers.

Phil smiled, leaning back in his seat. 'I wouldn't have given the go-ahead for this if I hadn't been confident that both of you can make it work very well...'

Stella had been unable to stop herself from looking forward to seeing Rob again on Friday afternoon, and it was making her very nervous about the possibility that he might make a last-minute decision not to turn up. But Reception had called, saying that Rob was on his way up, and Stella joined Phil in his office, sitting down in one of the comfortable chairs around a coffee table that was used for informal meetings. They waited in silence, and Stella jumped when a brisk knock sounded at the door.

Rob had clearly been making his own preparations for the meeting. Sunglasses weren't remarkable in this weather, but perched on the top of his head they made it look as if Rob was here on a social call. His light shoes, casual trousers and shirt were perfect for a summer evening with friends. And he'd grown a beard.

Not much of a beard, admittedly, but it was a good achievement for just six days. Well-trimmed and neat, and it suited him. If Stella had to sum up the overall look, *not here permanently* was the closest she could get.

'Rob!' Phil sprang to his feet, stepping forward to shake his hand. 'It's good to see you. You're looking well.'

'Thanks. It's good to be back.' Rob didn't sound quite as enthusiastic about the prospect as Phil did, but then he'd undoubtedly just run a gamut of curious glances and murmurs behind hands, because sunglasses and the shadow of a beard weren't really much of a disguise. Probably a few appreciative stares as well, given that he was looking particularly delicious today, even if that probably hadn't been his aim.

Phil waved him towards a chair, then made for the door to bellow for coffee. Stella was about to get to her feet, wondering whether shaking his hand was the right greeting, and Rob's sudden smile kept her in her seat. It had all the intimacy of an old friend.

'Hello again.' He sat down opposite her.

'Hello. Good journey here?' It was all that Stella could think of to say.

'Yeah. I left Sophie with Emma, they're keeping each other company for the afternoon. The fast trains into London from Hastings are pretty good.'

'Must be a little strange to be back...'

She saw his lip curl. Stella had learned what that meant at the weekend, and that Rob preferred not to bother with tact.

'Hard, you mean. Yeah, it is.'

'Right, then...' Phil interrupted the moment before Stella could reply, plumping himself down in a seat that was roughly equidistant from both of them and loosening his tie a notch. He had a way of making people feel comfortable around him, and Stella had learned that he did very little by chance. It was a gesture that was intended to bridge the gap between her smart trousers and jacket, and Rob's more casual look.

That wasn't needed. From the moment Rob had smiled, the connection was there, so strong that it was almost frightening.

'We'll get down to business, shall we?' Phil smiled at them both and Stella dragged her attention away from Rob. 'I'll be needing to know what role you feel you might take in this case, Rob.'

Nothing like cutting to the chase. Stella would like to know that too. Rob waved his hand in a gesture that intimated he wasn't too interested in roles.

'I was thinking of as and when Stella thinks I'm needed. On an informal basis.'

'Okay.' Phil gave Stella a querying look. It seemed that both he and Rob wanted her to take charge, and she didn't normally feel this flutter of uncertainty when that was required.

'Anna's case is one where we need to assess and integrate different skin repair techniques, and be prepared to apply them in new ways to provide a good result. We started to talk this through on Saturday, and I'd like to continue with those discussions and involve Rob in my planning of the surgery. Clearly Rob will need to see Anna in person, before we go too much further with either of those elements.'

Stella took a breath, wondering if either of the men was going to say anything, but neither did. So far so good, and this next part was where either Rob or Phil might have stronger opinions.

'It may well be beneficial for Rob to take some part in the surgery. What that part is depends largely on the outcome of our discussions, but also on how Rob feels about returning to surgery after a three-year break. We have some time before the date we've provisionally set for Anna's surgery, so can I suggest that we prepare for that possibility and make a joint decision on it later.'

Rob and Phil were both staring at her, and it was difficult to know what either of them was thinking. Then Phil spoke.

'I'm happy with that. What do you say, Rob?'

'Yep. Sounds good to me too.'

Phil beamed at them both. 'Right, then. And you're available on Thursdays and Fridays?'

'And every other weekend, when I'm not on call.'

'Weekends don't work for me.' Stella had thought about this and decided that she couldn't stop Rob from working weekends, but she wasn't going to facilitate it. He shot her a knowing smile, and she wondered whether she was in for a battle.

But he just shrugged. 'Okay. I can prune my fruit trees.'

Rob was too compliant. Maybe it was Phil's presence, or the fact that he was back here at the Thames Hospital, but Stella doubted that. Something else was coming...

'Anything we haven't covered?' Phil's innocent look told Stella that he was thinking the same as her.

A flash of steel showed in Rob's eyes, even though he was still smiling. 'As you know, I had my doubts about coming back to work here, but I can see how I might contribute to this particular case, and I'd like to help. I'm happy to work on a volunteer basis.'

'Wait...' Maybe Stella had missed something that had been understood between the two men, although she couldn't imagine that Phil would agree to that. It was irregular to say the least, and possibly even prohibited under the rules that governed the hospital's medical practice. 'When you say *volunteer*…?'

Phil nodded. 'My thoughts exactly. This hospital has plenty of volunteers, but I've never had a doctor in this department volunteering their services. Are we misunderstanding you, Rob?'

'Nope. You call on doctors with particular expertise all the time. I'm an NHS employee who has all of the necessary accreditation still in place, and this is the way I want to do things. If that's okay with you.'

This sounded a lot like *take it or leave it*. And from the creases that were forming on Phil's brow, it was a deal-breaker.

'I'm going to have to speak with HR…' That was Phil's usual get-out clause when he needed some time to think about something. Rob clearly knew that too, and he got to his feet.

'I'll let you do that…'

Phil looked up at him. 'Thanks, Rob. We do need to explore the options here. Where will you be?'

'Coffee bar. The one in the main building that used to do great pastries.'

'They still do…' Phil called after him as he made for the door, turning to Stella when Rob closed it quietly behind him.

Phil frowned in annoyance. 'This is Rob all over. He knows he's throwing a spanner into the works. We need to make sure that this is done properly and I'm not going to take any shortcuts or make Rob a special case, however much he wants to do things his way.'

Stella nodded, thinking hard. They'd gone through the motions with Rob, discussing avail-ability and what his role might be. But they hadn't talked about what really mattered: Rob's guilt, be-cause he felt he'd let everyone down. Phil's own feelings about what had happened three years ago.

'I've got a suggestion for a possible way for-ward...' If Stella couldn't find a compromise, then she very much doubted that Rob or Phil would be able to.

Maybe he'd gone too far... Rob hadn't thought too much about what he was going to say to Phil at their meeting, partly because he'd spent most of this week wondering exactly what he'd let him-self in for. And coming here had confirmed some of his fears. People remembered him, and three years ago they must have put two and two together and realised what had happened. He'd received only smiles and greetings, but in his mind they felt tainted with a past that he'd fought to leave behind.

It had left him off-balance. Wanting to turn and walk away, and knowing that if he did so he'd let Stella and Phil down. Maybe that was the real problem. Not letting them down today opened up a whole world of possible ways he might let them down in the future, and the idea weighed on his mind.

The coffee bar was just the same, situated in one corner of the large open-plan ground floor of the main building. There was always activity here, people walking from the entrance to the lifts, sometimes stopping for coffee or to browse the book exchange or visit the newsagent. And now that the midday rush was over there were plenty of seats, and he chose one in a corner by the window.

He'd ordered automatically, reaching into his pocket to pay while he was still absorbed in the choices that he'd already made, and those which lay ahead. Rob stared at the mug and plate in front of him. Coffee, with an extra shot to keep him alert, and a pastry as the quickest way to fill an empty stomach. That was what he'd always ordered three years ago, and he wondered whether herbal tea wouldn't be more in line with what he wanted—or maybe needed—now.

All the same, he sipped his coffee and took a bite from the pastry, the buzz of caffeine hitting him. Rob leaned back in his seat, another automatic reaction kicking in as he tried to relax before work claimed his concentration again. He made an effort to stop his fingers from tapping on the table in front of him, and tried to think about the open air and apple trees.

He was almost there—could almost see his orchard growing here in the heart of a city hospital, and feel the gentle rhythm of caring for trees instead of people—when he saw Stella walking towards him. He'd seen two sides of her on Saturday—a forthright, focused doctor, and a softer, more sensual woman, and there was no doubt which one was heading straight for him now.

Her hips had a businesslike sway to them, giving the sense that she knew exactly where she was going and was confident she'd get there. She sat down opposite him, looking at him thoughtfully for a moment. Her gaze seemed to burn into him.

'May I get you something?' Everything else seemed too hard at the moment, and Rob resorted to good manners. It was difficult to say the wrong thing when you were being scrupulously polite.

'No, thanks. I've just been drinking coffee with Phil.' Stella's smile never quite managed to conceal her allure, despite her professional appearance. The combination of the two was tempting in the extreme, and he felt caught now, in the heat of her gaze.

'Here's how it's going to be, Rob.'

He nodded. Rob reckoned that was about all a man could do when faced with Stella at her most determined.

'I know that coming here hasn't been easy for you...'

'You understand that?' Despite her apparent ability to put herself in his shoes, he was pretty sure that she didn't appreciate the finer points of it.

'No, I don't, because I haven't been through what you have and had the guts to come back from it. I have an imagination, though.'

Good answer. And Stella didn't pull any punches. He liked that about her, because she couldn't possibly hurt him any more than he'd hurt himself, with the constant reproach and guilt. And her no-nonsense attitude made him feel better about what he was feeling now. He nodded, and felt that sudden connection between them. That was challenging too, but meeting it head-on made him feel a little stronger.

'You need an opportunity to go with the flow a little, and ease yourself back into the hospital's routine. Phil needs to run a department, and that means knowing what to expect from everyone at any given time...'

That was a pretty good summary of the situation. Rob opened his mouth to concur, and Stella silenced him with a wave of her finger. Clearly even his agreement wasn't necessary at the moment.

'So this is what I propose. For ten hours a week you're welcome here in the department, doing whatever you want to do, on a voluntary basis. You can have as much coffee as you like with whoever you like, scrub up to observe a few surgical procedures...' She waved her hand to encompass many possible options. 'Since we're a teaching hospital you can even collar a few of our students and point them in the right direction.'

That sounded like something he could live with. There was obviously more coming and Rob swallowed his agreement and confined himself to a nod.

'You lay one finger on a patient, attend a planning meeting or read a file, and you're on the clock. Phil can get HR to draw up a contract for ten hours a week, in addition to the hours you spend volunteering.'

'Two shifts a week.' Rob couldn't help noticing that Stella's own contribution to the discussions was incorporated, and that he probably wouldn't be getting any chance to add weekends to his work schedule.

'Not necessarily full shifts. We can negotiate with you over the times we need you, and you organise your volunteering however you want, that's up to you. You're in control of part of your time, but you allow us to depend on you to be there when we need you. Can you commit yourself to that?'

*Really* commit himself. Rob was under no illusions about that, because Stella's focus didn't brook any half measures. But she'd come up with a plan that allowed him to feel his way back into a challenging situation, and still have the rewards of participating in the demanding work of the department. And he reckoned that Stella would get what she wanted too.

'Are you happy with it?'

She smiled suddenly. 'I want you on my team.'

'Okay. You have a deal…' He offered his hand to shake hers.

'You're sure? This is binding, Rob.'

*Don't let me down.*

That was her meaning, but for once Stella didn't come straight out and say it. But she'd already suggested a framework where he could feel confident that he wouldn't let her down.

'As soon as we shake on it, it's set in stone.' He threw back his own challenge, and saw the spark of excitement in her face that he always felt when faced with a testing situation.

There was a touch of the playful about the way that her fingers drew back a little before meeting his. Something delicious, that made their final contact all the more meaningful. Stella shook his hand and then gave him a smile, taking her phone from her pocket and starting to type with both thumbs.

'Okay…ten hours volunteering…ten hours working. Have you thought about an hourly rate…?'

'That doesn't matter, does it?' This was all about recognising his fears over being able to fit back into a situation that had once broken him.

'No, I suppose not. I dare say HR can sort out those details…' Stella shot him a smile. 'It's not really the money, is it? As soon as Phil puts you on the payroll, all of the checks and balances and safeguarding procedures kick in. That's the real point, for both of you.'

She saw that. Rob had too, and Phil obviously had, but Stella had broken it down and made something workable out of it. She finished typing and then put her phone down on the table, picking it up again when it vibrated.

'Okay, Phil was clearly staring at his phone, waiting for my text... He says that's fine.' Her phone vibrated again in her hand. 'And... He's off to twist a few arms in the HR department and your contract should be ready for you to review by the end of the day.'

'That's great, thanks. Does that mean I can call you *boss* now?' The sudden resolution of a problem that had been bugging him all week allowed the joke.

'Not until you know me better,' Stella flashed back. '*Stella* will do for the time being.'

Rob chuckled. 'Right you are. Any chance of staying around for the rest of the afternoon? I'll pick the contract up from Phil when it's ready and sign it.'

'Absolutely. Remember Prof Maitland?'

'Of course.' Everyone knew Alma Maitland— she'd been teaching here for thirty years, and it was no surprise to Rob that she was still refusing to retire.

'Well, I just so happen to have noticed...' Stella's

grin told Rob that she'd made a point of looking it up '...that she's doing a tutorial on suture techniques this afternoon. She never minds a bit of teaching assistance from anyone who happens to be at a loose end.' Stella left the suggestion hanging in the air between them.

'I'll pop in and see her, and ask whether I can sit in. Phil first, though, just to confirm my agreement to everything.'

'Yeah, that would be good.' Stella picked up her phone, typing another text. 'You feel as if you've let him down, don't you. Did you realise that he feels he's let *you* down?'

That hadn't occurred to Rob. 'Phil never let me down. He did all he could to help when I was working here, and after I left he was the only person who stayed in touch.'

'That doesn't surprise me. But how we feel about a situation isn't always a reflection of how things actually are.'

Message received, loud and clear. 'Maybe it's time for me to thank him, for all the support he's given me. Clear the air a bit.'

Stella nodded, leaving it at that. Her phone buzzed and she picked it up. 'Ah, that's Alma. She says you're to get your gorgeously rounded intellect up to her office before she has to send out a search party.'

Rob chuckled. Clearly, Alma hadn't changed. 'I don't have her number in my phone. Could you tell her twenty minutes, after I've had a chance to see Phil.'

Stella smiled, typing a reply. 'I don't suppose you have time for something to eat before you go back home tonight?' After all of the hard questions they'd just faced, this was the one that prompted a sudden diffidence in her tone.

And it was the question that Rob had wanted to ask too. 'Six o'clock? My shout.'

'You can pay for mine and I'll pay for yours.'

It was an elegant twist on splitting the bill, but Rob was under no illusions that he'd just hit a brick wall. Stella's frankness felt very intimate at times, and she clearly cared about the people around her. But she drew a hard line between friendship and even the smallest hint of anything closer. Rob did too, but he couldn't help stumbling over it from time to time when he was in Stella's company.

'Fair enough. I'll do my best to work up a healthy appetite.'

Stella chuckled, getting to her feet and picking up her phone. Whatever was next on her agenda seemed to be beckoning. 'You haven't seen my to-do list for the afternoon. I'll be ravenous by six o'clock.'

On a Friday evening in summer, every pub and eatery on the banks of the Thames was full to bursting. Stella had given a bit of thought to the matter and decided against being squashed against a whole crowd of people she didn't know, and having to shout to make herself heard.

They'd stopped off at the new fish and chip shop by the hospital, and then walked towards the river, finding a place to sit on a set of wide steps that led down to the embankment. Spreading the bag out between them, she arranged the tub of tomato sauce and sachets of salt and vinegar on it and then opened the paper wrappings around her fish and chips.

'Mmm. Really good chips. The fish is nice too.' Rob was a little ahead of her, obviously hungry. 'If that place had been open when I worked here, I wouldn't have got so thin...'

He could make a wry joke about it now, even if it was accompanied by a downward quirk of his lips. That seemed to be a good sign.

'How was Alma's tutorial?'

Rob chuckled. 'Pretty much as you'd expect. She took a brisk hop through the theory and then threw me in at the deep end along with her students, and told them that if they were going to pass muster they needed to be able to emulate what I was about to demonstrate.'

'And how did everyone do?' Stella knew the answer to that already. Alma was notorious for making sure that no one in her tutorial group got left behind, and no doubt Rob had found himself in the shadow of that over-arching principle as well.

'It needed a few tries, but they got there. And a

few of them stayed around to ask questions afterwards. It's nice to be around all of that enthusiasm again. And I'm glad to find that I can still suture with ten pairs of eyes trained on my every move.'

He seemed pleased. And he had an envelope, stowed away in the inside pocket of his jacket, which contained his copy of the contract that Phil had given him before they'd left this evening, which Rob had read through and signed straight away.

'Including Alma's?'

He nodded. 'Yeah, she was right at the front of the group, watching every move I made. If she didn't correct me, then I reckon I can't be too rusty. How was your afternoon?'

'Good. After finding a way of making you and Phil see eye to eye, a couple of surgical scar reductions were a piece of cake.'

'I'm sure they were. You're not a middle child, are you?'

'As it happens, yes. You think that makes me a mediator?'

That wasn't what Rob was asking. She knew a great deal about him, and now Rob wanted to know something about her. The thought made Stella smile.

'I wouldn't reduce it to that.' He picked up one of the sachets, opening it and then sprinkling his chips with salt. Clearly waiting to see whether Stella would respond to his invitation.

ANNIE CLAYDON                    67

'I have an older sister and a younger brother. Chloe's married with three children, and Jamie and his wife have a little boy. They all get on very well together, and so there's not much call for mediation.'

'Nice. I like nephews and nieces, I have a few of them too. I'd show you the pictures only my fingers are getting a bit greasy.'

There was a trace of regret in his smile. It struck a chord somewhere in Stella's own heart. 'The road not travelled?'

Rob nodded. 'Yeah. There are a few of them. I never got to be a newsreader, or a sea captain either.'

'You wanted to be a newsreader?'

He shrugged. 'It was a phase. When I was eight years old, I thought that sitting behind a huge desk and knowing everything that was going on in the world must be wonderful. Then it occurred to me that it would be better to actually *see* all of the places they were talking about, and decided on sea captain. It was touch and go between that and a pilot for a while, and then I decided on surgery.'

'I only ever wanted to be a surgeon...' Suddenly Stella wished that she'd at least thought about being something else. Ballerina maybe. Or a pilot sounded like a good ambition to have for a while, and then leave behind in favour of the one you really wanted. 'My dad's a surgeon, and so I got hooked on the idea pretty early.'

'So you were pretty focused, even when you were a child.'

Stella couldn't work out whether that was a criticism or a compliment. 'There's nothing wrong with focus, is there?'

'Not a thing.' Rob turned the corners of his mouth down. 'It does tend to mess with everything else, though.'

'No one said that being a surgeon means that you can't have a life. My mum and dad wanted different things and that made them a great team. Dad wasn't around much when we were little, but we understood why and knew that he was doing important work. And Mum was always there for us.'

'So it's all a matter of finding the right person?' Rob seemed to be turning the idea over in his head.

They were straying into territory that made Stella feel uncomfortable. Rob's relationship with his ex-wife was his own business, and talking about it felt like stepping over a line that shouldn't be crossed.

'I'm no expert on marriage.'

He laughed suddenly. 'You think *I* am? I'm not looking for any answers, I'm just interested in what you think.'

'I just know that my mum and dad made things work because they'd both made their own choices about what they wanted from life, and they were each doing what they wanted to do. When I applied for medical school, Dad sat me down and told me that it wasn't going to be easy…'

'And that prepared you?' Rob raised an eyebrow.

'What do you think? I knew that studying medicine was going to take commitment, but I still had to find out what that really meant. I did that the hard way, like everyone else. I had my share of boyfriends who just walked away because I was studying when they wanted to go out. Had my heart broken…' Stella pressed her lips together. That sounded as if her whole life, every decision she'd made, had been a reaction to having been hurt.

'In my experience, young men of that age can be foolish.' Rob murmured the words quietly. It was tempting to pretend that she hadn't heard them, because they opened a door that had remained shut for some time.

But she *had* heard, and it made her feel good. Made her want things that she knew she couldn't have.

'It is what it is. I've made my choices about what I want out of life, and I focus on the things that I care about. I don't give untravelled roads too much thought.' She grinned at him. 'They're probably full of potholes, anyway.'

'I envy you your certainty.'

Stella's grip on that certainty was beginning to loosen. But a warm evening, spent with a man who was both emotionally intelligent and unsettlingly attractive, was just a passing temptation. It wasn't a reason to make any sudden, uncontrolled changes in direction.

They sat, watching the boats travel up and down the river, finishing the last of their chips. Rob screwed the wrapping paper into a ball, tossing it restlessly from one hand to the other, while Stella folded hers neatly.

'So what's on your agenda for the weekend?' he asked.

Probably best not to mention that she was thinking of popping in to work tomorrow. Stella told him about the family lunch at her parents' house on Sunday, and showed him the pictures of her nephews and nieces on her phone. Rob reciprocated with pictures of a cute little girl, whose grey-blue eyes were just as mesmerising as his, and two older boys. When questioned about his weekend, he laughed.

'The thing about gardens is that you just go out there and they tell you what needs to be done, rather than the other way around.' He looked at his watch, pulling the corners of his mouth down. 'I should get going. My train's in twenty minutes.'

Stella nodded, picking up her bag and threading the strap across her shoulder. 'Thanks for dinner.'

'Thank *you*.'

Parting was strange and awkward. It deserved some acknowledgement of the confidences they'd exchanged, but a kiss on the cheek was too intimate. A handshake too formal. But when Stella looked up into his face, Rob's smile and the look in his eyes was just right. Warm, almost tender, and above all unspoken. She turned, taking that smile with her, as she walked away.

# CHAPTER FIVE

STELLA HAD DECIDED that this was positively the last time that she would allow herself to miss Rob for the five days that he was down in Sussex. Next week she'd barely think about him. Rob had turned up at the hospital bright and early on Thursday morning, putting his head around her office door to announce his presence.

'Am I back on the clock?'

'Yes.' Stella smiled at him, pushing Anna's patient file across the desk.

Anna was due in for a consultation at half past nine, which would give Rob a chance to meet her and examine her injuries. And Stella wanted to revisit her discussions with Anna about what she wanted from her surgery, in the light of the possibilities and techniques that she and Rob had already considered.

'Does Anna have any clear idea about her own priorities?' Rob asked as Stella made a list of talking points.

'She's a little overwhelmed by it all at the moment and I'd really like to get her to see that she's in control of the process, and what she wants matters to us. Maybe if we start with your examination, and then we can bring that around to a more general discussion?' Stella didn't want to be too proscriptive about who did what, and she was happy to allow Rob to lead the session while she sat in, ready to take over if necessary.

'You know her best.' He gave her a dazzling smile. 'I don't want to step on your toes…'

Stella didn't want that either. It implied the kind of physical closeness that would make her forget about crushed toes, and think only about pulling him a little closer.

'We'll see how it goes, shall we? Work from there…' Her phone buzzed and she picked it up. 'Anna and Jess are a little early, they're here already…'

Rob was quite capable of insisting that everything went his way. But the way that he spoke with Anna and her partner, Jess, left neither of them in any doubt that his whole focus was making sure that they went Anna's way. Right from the start, he was gentle and encouraging, listening to everything that Anna said and taking careful notes. And then suddenly he swerved off script.

'How we see ourselves is entirely personal. It's inconsequential, but I have a bit of a thing about the bump on my nose…'

There wasn't anything wrong with the bump on his nose. Stella quite liked it. One slight imperfection in an otherwise perfect face. And mentioning it seemed a little tactless—until Rob shot Jess a querying glance, and Stella realised that he'd read Anna and Jess perfectly...

'The bump's fine. You could get rid of the stubble, though.' Jess was always the more forthright of the two.

'Jess!' Anna shot her partner a reproving look. 'Don't listen to her, the beard's fine. It makes you look less like a doctor.'

Rob nodded, scraping his fingers across his chin. 'Glad you think so. To be honest with you, that was why I grew it in the first place.' Anna and Jess couldn't know the reasons behind that, but the vulnerability that showed in Rob's eyes couldn't be manufactured.

And it broke the ice. Anna began to talk, and this time she was using her own likes and dislikes as a guide. Rob answered all of her questions, giving her an honest appraisal of what could and couldn't be done.

'So...before we go can I just ask...' Jess had one more question, and Rob turned to her, grinning.

'Absolutely. Ask away.'

'Who's going to be doing Anna's surgery?'

'Ms Parry-Jones.' Rob didn't miss a beat. 'She's the senior surgeon for Anna's case and she'll be making all of the decisions with you.'

Jess and Anna looked at each other. Clearly Rob's quiet but authoritative manner had impressed them both, and they were wondering who this new person on their radar was.

'My role is technical consultant. Ms Parry-Jones has asked me to provide input on a few specialised aspects of your case, Anna, so that she can give you the best all-round care.'

'Right… Okay, thanks.' Jess seemed happy with the answer, but Stella couldn't leave it at that.

'Mr Franklin has specific expertise in the reduction of scars like the one you have on your forehead, Anna. His input is going to be particularly useful there.' Anna had mentioned that the way that the scar was pulling at her eyelid bothered her.

'That's great. Thank you so much, both of you.' Anna seemed much more confident about the process that lay ahead of her now.

Jess gathered up their coats, waiting for Anna to say her goodbyes. When the door closed behind the two women Rob turned to Stella, a reproachful smile on his face.

'You didn't need to say that.'

'Yes, I did. Anna has a right to know that she has excellent people on her team.' And Rob had a right to know that his own expertise was valued. 'Did Phil give you that job title?'

'No. I made it up on the spur of the moment. What do you think of it?'

She thought that Rob was probably trying to make a point. 'It's a little self-effacing, isn't it? You could have just said that you were a surgeon working on Anna's case.'

'I'm not wholly comfortable with that at the moment. I'll go with technical consultant for the time being.'

'And a beard.'

He shrugged. 'Opinion appears to be split on the beard. I don't suppose you'd like to exercise your casting vote?'

'No, I wouldn't. I don't suppose that all of this has anything to do with letting me know that you're not here to challenge me, does it?'

He shrugged. 'You're the one who doesn't like it when I call you *boss*. But if you'd like me to remind you that you're in charge, then I can work it into the conversation whenever I get the chance.'

Stella puffed out an exasperated breath. 'I wouldn't want to put words into your mouth. I suppose that being in charge of Anna's case doesn't extend to me asking what you're up to for the rest of the day.'

Rob gave her a delicious smile, getting to his feet. 'Right in one. Largely because I'm off the clock now, and I'm not entirely sure myself.'

Stella had been meaning to ask Rob whether he'd like to scrub up for the procedure to correct Dupuytren's contracture that she was carrying out at one o'clock. Releasing the thick bands of tissue that bent the fingers and restricted movement was a relatively straightforward process, and Stella was under no illusions that she had anything to teach him about it. But an hour in Theatre, even if he was only observing, might make Rob think a little more about including surgery in his job description. Since she couldn't find him at lunchtime, she decided that the conversation could wait.

The surgery went well, and when her patient was wheeled through to the recovery room Stella scrubbed out, flipping through the messages on her phone as she waited for the lift to take her back to her office.

'There's a facial injury in A&E?' She stopped in the open doorway of the department's admin offices, and Sadie, who always knew where everyone was at any given time, looked up from her computer screen.

'Don't worry about that one. Mr Franklin's dealing with it.'

'Okay. Thanks, Sadie.'

*Don't run. Not even if your heart's pounding and you're wondering if Rob has just broken every promise he made, and gone completely rogue...*

All the same, Stella hit the lifts at a very brisk walking pace, and was a little out of breath by the time she entered A&E. The senior doctor was standing at the admin station, and looked up from a tablet.

'Hey, Stella. No one told me that this was Visit Your Emergency Doctor Day.' Therese grinned at her.

'Sorry. No one told me either. I don't suppose

you've seen Rob Franklin down here, have you?'
Stella slowed down, shooting her a smile.

'I've seen everyone—Rob Franklin, Phil Chamberlain, now you. Must be a slow day for the Reconstructive Surgery department...' Therese reached over to answer the phone, mouthing an apology.

Okay. If Phil was here, then maybe she should just turn around and go back upstairs, because he would be dealing with the situation. Then she saw Phil emerging from one of the cubicles and heading towards her.

'Thanks for coming down, Stella. Rob's just going through a few aftercare points with a patient, and I've had a call from the ward and I need to go back up there.'

'So everything's under control, then.' Now would be a very good time to go, before Rob got the impression that she was stalking him.

'Uh... Wait...' Therese had finished her conversation and was now replacing the phone back into its cradle. 'Is there any chance of one of you being able to stay? A young man's just walked in with a series of lacerations to his shoulder, which are bleeding profusely. He's with a doctor now, and we're doing scans to find out exactly what's going on, but we may be calling you to ask if you're able to come back down again any minute now.'

Phil nodded. 'I can get someone to cover for you upstairs, Stella.'

'I've just finished the Dupuytren's contracture

surgery, and I need someone to look in on that patient when he's out of the recovery room. Then I have ward rounds...'

'I can take care of that. You stay here and work with Rob.' Phil didn't give any room for an answer, let alone a disagreement, and hurried away.

'You can relax.' Therese mistook Stella's look of discomfiture for lack of confidence in Rob's abilities. 'He's as good as he ever was. Better, maybe—he seems to have developed his interpersonal skills.'

Working as a GP would do that. And Therese had been here for some years, she must be in a position to see the difference. 'He's been away for a while, though.'

Therese nodded. Everyone understood the need to go carefully until they were sure that Rob's extended absence hadn't affected his performance in any way. That was for Rob's sake as well as being a safeguarding measure for their patients.

'Don't go telling me that he's better than I am...' The thought that had been nagging at Stella slipped out. She knew Therese well enough that it wouldn't go any further than just the two of them.

'No, it's not like that.' Therese grinned. 'Apples and pears, you know?'

Stella wondered whether she should mention that she'd mistaken one of Rob's pear trees for an apple tree, and decided not to. Therese could see the differences better than most, and she worked outside the Reconstructive Surgery Unit, so had nothing to gain or lose in comparing Rob's performance with hers. *Apples and pears* was the best answer she was going to get from anyone.

'Got to go...' Therese was already on the move, leaving Stella alone by the admin station. A&E was always busy and wasting time talking about fruit, and her own private misgivings, wasn't helpful. And Stella reminded herself that losing her focus wasn't helpful either.

She should keep that thought uppermost in her mind. When she knocked and opened the door to the cubicle she'd seen Phil emerge from, focus seemed suddenly impossible.

Rob was sitting opposite the patient couch, talking to a young boy in school football kit and his mother. He'd found one of the patient leaflets and had clearly been taking the mother through aftercare for cuts and stitches, while keeping the boy amused with stick figures drawn in the margin. The first was clutching its head and Rob had covered the whole procedure, through to his own ministrations in stitching the wound.

'And you say there won't be a scar?' the mother asked, grinning at her son's delight over the final stick figure, which had a broad smile on its face and seemed to be kicking a football.

'There will be—but just a hairline. It'll be barely noticeable and David's young so it may well disappear completely in time.'

Just a glance at the stitches on the side of the boy's face was enough to tell her that Rob's estimate was correct. It had clearly been a nasty cut and the droplets of blood falling from the head of the first stick figure were probably no exaggeration. But she couldn't fault the treatment of the wound, it was exactly what she would have done. Better than she could have done, maybe. Apples and pears…

'If you see any signs of infection, you need to either go to your GP or come back here and get someone to look at it.' He handed the guidance leaflet to the mother, and the boy grabbed it from her, getting a special smile from Rob. 'And David. Less tackling with your head and more with your feet when you're playing football, eh? You're not going to score a winning goal by landing up in A&E, are you?'

David shook his head, and responded to his mother's nudged prompt. 'Thank you, Dr Rob.'

'My pleasure, David.' Rob produced another leaflet for David's mother, and she stowed it away in her handbag. Her son clearly wanted to stay here with Rob, and she practically had to drag him away, thanking Rob again and smiling at Stella as she left the cubicle.

'You've taken over nursemaid duties?' The warmth was still in Rob's face, and the twinkle of humour in his eyes was almost irresistible.

'I wouldn't say that.'

'No, you wouldn't.' He got to his feet, and suddenly his bulk seemed impressive in the small space. 'That's *my* interpretation. I was the one who was cautious about coming back, remember? The joke's on me.'

Stella wondered whether anyone who'd known Rob when he'd worked here three years ago would be surprised at finding he had become the butt of his own jokes. That was irrelevant, because the present was what mattered.

'There's a new patient with lacerations to his shoulder. They're controlling the bleeding and doing preliminary scans right now.'

Rob nodded. 'No point in going back upstairs then, if we get paged in the lift.'

'Yep...' Stella's phone beeped and she pulled it out of her pocket, looking at the message. 'Cubicle Ten.'

Moving, having something to do, clarified everything. There was no more time to appreciate his broad shoulders and the precise deftness of his hands. To think that while patients must find his touch very reassuring, she could imagine his hands provoking a far more erotic response. There was no more uncertainty over meeting Rob's gaze and she could focus now. Stella led the way to one of the larger cubicles, situated next to the trauma unit, which was equipped to handle patients who needed minor surgical interventions.

The young man lying on the bed was conscious,

his gaze taking in everything that was going on around him. A nurse was dealing with a mess of bloodstained clothing and dressings and their patient's pallor, emphasised by his freckled face and shock of red hair, was another indication of blood loss. Stella remembered Therese's words—'*just walked in*'. How could anyone, let alone someone who looked so young, walk very far with these injuries?

She turned to the doctor in attendance, seeing relief in her eyes as she rapped out the details. 'This is Matthew Jarvis, he's seventeen years old. He has lacerations to his right shoulder and upper arm, and there's been significant blood loss, but we have that under control now. We've set up a live X-ray and ultrasound, and I don't see any indication that the lacerations are deep.'

'Okay, thanks.' Seventeen. That was too young, and Matthew looked like a child, surrounded by the medical equipment that was being used to scan his wounds. She turned to the live X-ray screen, studying it carefully.

'What do you think?' She'd already made her decision about what should come next, but asking Rob allowed him to make the formal diagnosis. The twitch of his lips showed that he saw exactly what she was doing, and the warmth in his face told her that he was grateful. He looked at the X-ray screen before moving on to the ultrasound, adjusting the sensors so that they could see the full extent of the long cuts on Matthew's shoulder and arm and assess their depth.

'It doesn't look as if any of the tendons or muscles have been compromised, and there's nothing in the wounds. They all look relatively shallow.' Rob turned to the lad. 'How did this happen, Matthew?'

'It's Matt.' The boy's face twisted into an expression of bravado, which only made him look even younger. 'There were some kids in the shopping precinct, playing with knives. I went to take 'em off them.'

'That's very public-spirited. What kind of knives?' Rob's face gave no indication of his thoughts.

'They were like hunting knives. A bloke came to help and he took charge of them. The kids ran away when he said he was calling the police. I didn't realise they'd cut me at first, but when I saw the blood someone brought me here.'

'They brought you in?'

'Nah, he dropped me off in the car park. He gave me a lift, but he said he had errands.'

There was something about this that didn't quite ring true. Stella had seen pretty much every kind of wound that it was possible to inflict and the ultrasound scans indicated that Matthew's injuries had been caused by something with a short blade, like a box-cutter, not a long-bladed knife. And Stella couldn't imagine that many people would drive a badly injured young man to hospital and then leave him in the car park, however many other things they had to do.

Stella glanced up at Rob and when his gaze met hers for a moment she could see her own thoughts reflected in his eyes. Matthew was lying about something, and when that something involved knives it made everyone in a hospital particularly careful.

'Okay. Thanks.' Rob turned his attention back to the screens, studying them carefully.

'What do you reckon?' Stella prompted him again.

'I think do a visual check, and then close the wounds. I don't see any evidence of other damage that would need to be repaired surgically.'

'I agree.' For all of the precision of the medical equipment around them, their own experience and the look of a wound was still a valuable part of their assessment. She picked up the patient notes, writing one word in the margin and showing it to Rob.

*Security?*

He nodded. 'My thoughts exactly. You go and speak with Therese.'

Rob's tone brooked no argument. Stella supposed that it made sense. He would stay with the duty doctor and the two nurses who were tending to Matthew, while she raised their concerns with Therese. All the same, there was a protectiveness in his manner, and he shot her a smile before he moved towards Matthew, asking whether he might take a look at his shoulder, and gently easing back the dressings from one of the wounds. The A&E doctor stepped back, out of Rob's way, as did both of the nurses, and Stella hurried from the cubicle to find Therese.

# CHAPTER SIX

WHAT MATTHEW HAD said didn't add up, and Rob had a strong feeling that something wasn't right. He and Stella didn't even need to speak about it; the guidelines about how they should deal with this kind of situation were clear. It was best to err on the side of caution and there would be no questions asked if they requested that one of the security guards who worked in A&E be stationed outside the door of the cubicle in case he was needed. With security guard Terry in place outside the door, Stella returned to the cubicle and she and Rob went ahead and treated their patient in just the same way as they would any other.

Rob had made sure that anything which might be construed as a weapon was out of Matthew's reach. The lad wasn't particularly talkative, but then the level of analgesic that had been needed before they embarked on stitching the four long gashes on his shoulder and arm was enough to make anyone a little drowsy.

This was what Rob had lived for, once upon a time. This level of challenge. It had usually been dictated by the medical difficulties involved in a particular patient's case, but although his gut feeling that something wasn't quite right here was very different, it produced the same heightened awareness. The same feeling he'd clung to when he'd been working here at the hospital three years ago.

'That's it, Matt. All done.' Stella gave Matthew a dazzling smile, telling him he'd done well. Rob had had better patients—Matthew had grumbled about the time that the stitches were taking—but he'd had worse as well. And he was back. He knew now that he'd lost none of his edge and that he'd completed the complex closure of the intersecting wounds with the same skill that he'd been able to command three years ago. Stella didn't need to tell him that, although he hoped she might later on.

'Can I go now?' Matthew sat up, wincing as he tried to use his right arm.

'Not yet.' She picked up a pair of surgical scissors. 'I need to trim some of the stitches and then we'll dress your arm and give you a sling to use for the next few days. Is there someone at home who can look after you?'

'Yeah. My mum. I should really go now—she's expecting me and she'll be worried.'

'Can you phone her? Perhaps she'll come and collect you.'

'Nah, she never answers her phone. I'll be all right.'

'Well, perhaps we can get you a taxi when we're finished here. I don't think you should go home on your own. And there's something else I want to talk to you about as well...'

Matthew's attitude so far had largely been one of irritation that everything was taking so long. Rob had been keeping a close eye on him but, although he wasn't being particularly cooperative, he hadn't shown any hostility towards them. He allowed himself to move back a little to sort through the dressings they'd need, reckoning that if Stella's smile couldn't get through to Matthew, then nothing would.

'We have a social worker attached to the hospital who's available to speak with anyone who's been involved in an incident with knives. If you'd like me to give her a call and see if she's available I can do that now.'

'No. I can't be bothered with social workers.'

'Okay. But I think we should also report this to the police. Your injuries are fairly significant, and they may want to speak with you.'

'No police.'

'It's important, Matt.' This had to be said, and Stella's tone contained no hint of a challenge. But something had made the hairs on the back of Rob's neck rise, and he turned to glance across at her.

'No police!' Matthew became suddenly aggressive, and Stella yelped in surprise as he snatched the surgical scissors from her hand, winding his arm around her neck and dragging her back against him.

'Matt. Put the scissors down.' Rob heard his own voice, calm in the face of his raging anger and his fear for Stella.

'No police. And get out of the way. I want to leave now.'

'I'm afraid I can't. Not until you put the scissors down and let my colleague go. All she's done is try to help you, Matt.'

'She wants to call the police. And I'm out of here, now.'

'Whether or not we call the police about your injuries is your choice. But if you hurt anyone here, or take one step outside this room with those scissors in your hand, then everything changes. You won't have any choices.'

It was already too late for ifs. One tear had escaped from Stella's frightened eyes and even though Rob could see that she was trying to hold herself together she was terrified. Matthew had already hurt her, but Rob had to concentrate on making him believe that he had a way out of this.

The panic button was only two steps away, but he couldn't risk it. Matthew was pressing the scissors against Stella's neck now, and she whimpered as she felt the cold steel against her skin. The outside edges of the scissors were rounded and designed not to cut, but she had no way of knowing which side of the blade she could feel.

'Put the scissors down, Matt. Let her go.'

'Then what?'

'Then I'll dress your wound and give you a sling. After that, you'll be released and you can go wherever you want.' That was a downright lie. But Rob would swear that up was down and dance on the ceiling to prove it if that got Stella away from Matthew.

'All right. Just give me the sling, I don't need anything more. And I'll go straight away.'

'Not until you let her go, Matt. That's the way it works. I can't do anything for you until you do that.'

The scissors clattered onto the floor, and suddenly Stella was in his arms. Rob's first and only instinct was to get her away from Matthew, and he pulled the door open, bundling her out of the cubicle. Terry, the security guard who'd been sitting outside the door, jumped to his feet.

Rob hadn't forgotten the procedure; it was ingrained in everyone who'd ever worked here. Standing in the doorway so that he could keep an eye on Matthew, he quickly relayed the code for an assault on a member of staff. Terry nodded, speaking quietly into his radio to alert the security centre for the building.

'Step back now, please.' Terry was one of the most amiable people it was possible to meet, but when he gestured to Rob to stand to one side and moved into the doorway, his sheer size was enough to get Matthew to sit back down on the bed, clutching his shoulder and grunting in pain.

And Rob could do the one thing he'd been aching to do, and concentrate on Stella now, knowing that the situation with Matthew was under control. She clung to him and he put his arm around her shoulders, trying to comfort her. Then he saw her hand move to her neck, her fingers searching…

'You're okay, Stella. He didn't cut you. He was pressing the blunt side of the scissors against your skin.'

'I thought…' Stella tried for a smile and failed miserably. 'Silly…'

'No, it's not silly at all. You couldn't possibly have known that. Just hold tight for a moment, we'll be out of here soon.'

He could see a ripple of concern move through the A&E staff as the alert went out. Another guard came hurrying towards them, along with one of the male doctors, and they joined Terry as he walked almost casually into the cubicle, closing the door behind them.

The work of the department carried on, doctors and nurses doing their best to preserve an atmosphere of calm and control. It felt to Rob as if he'd just woken from a bad dream, adrenaline still coursing in his veins, but nowhere to run and nothing to do.

'Rob…make sure he's all right… Don't let anyone hurt him.' Stella clutched at his arm, her fingers pressing tight.

'No one's going to hurt Matthew. They're making sure that everyone's safe, him included.' Stella knew that as well as he did, it was just the adrenaline talking.

Therese was hurrying towards them now, a look of concern on her face. 'Are you guys okay?'

'Yes.' Stella broke free of him, almost pushing him away. Her sudden air of composure was the most worrying reaction she could have displayed. 'I'm just going upstairs for a moment.'

Stella didn't wait for an answer before starting to walk towards the exit. 'She's in shock.' Therese stated the obvious. 'I'll go.'

Rob watched as Therese caught up with her, and the two women walked together towards the double doors that led through to the A&E reception area and the lifts. He knew that Therese would look after Stella, but couldn't help wishing that he was the one at Stella's side right now.

But Stella had asked him to make sure that Matthew was all right. He was still a doctor, and there was a job here for him to finish before he went to find Stella. Rob shook his head, turning reluctantly towards the door of the cubicle.

Every moment that Rob was away from Stella felt like an age, but in truth it took little more than half an hour to hand over to the A&E doctor, then give his account of what had happened to the police. Therese arrived back in A&E, beckoning him

into an empty cubicle, and closing the door behind them.

'How's Stella?'

Therese sat down in one of the chairs, and
waited until Rob sat down in the other. He was
pretty sure that she did that with most of her patients, there was something about sitting down together that changed the nature of a conversation.

'She's obviously shaken up. But she's okay and
she'll deal with it in her own way.'

Rob nodded, taking a breath. 'Which is?'

'Well, at the moment that takes the form of sitting in her office and pretending to do some work.
I made her a cup of tea and stayed with her while
the police took a brief statement. Phil Chamberlain's keeping an eye on her, now.'

'So…she's on her own?'

'That's what she wanted, Rob. Give her some
time to think it all through and then she might just
work out that she's not to blame for all of this.'

'It's not Stella's fault. It's mine…' Rob ignored
Therese's eyeroll. 'If I'd been quicker, I could have
stopped him.'

'Will you listen to yourself? It's not Stella's
fault and it's not yours either. We deal with people in crisis every day, and these things happen.
The main thing is that no one was hurt.' Therese
frowned at him and Rob puffed out a breath.

'So I'm acting like an idiot?' Rob had always

liked and respected Therese, and that was what she clearly thought.

'Yes and no. Yes, because you very clearly aren't to blame, and no because with twenty/twenty hindsight it's natural to feel there's something you could have done to prevent what happened.' Therese leaned forward, clearly intent on catching his attention. 'That's why it's hospital policy to make a counsellor available to any staff members who are involved in incidents like this.'

'I don't need...' Rob stopped himself before he fell into that trap. 'I expect that's what Stella said as well.'

'Not quite. Stella finished the sentence. At least you have the wit to see that the policy's there for a reason.'

Rob leaned back in his seat. There was something about sitting down and being on the sharp end of Therese's common sense. 'I know what happens when you try to bottle things up. First-hand.'

'Yes, you do. I don't think I ever said how sorry I was about what happened to you, Rob. It's really good to see you back.'

'I didn't give anyone the chance to help me, and I really regret that. It's good to be back.' Rob knew exactly what he needed to do now. He was living, breathing proof of the way that stress could quietly build until it was a force that could destroy a person. And he was back now, and that had to mean something.

Therese nodded. 'You'll be around for a while?'

'Long enough to buy you a beer one evening… if I'm not too late in asking?' Maybe he'd burned all of his bridges three years ago, when he'd left without a word to anyone.

'You'll throw in a packet of crisps?' Therese grinned at him.

'Done.' Rob got to his feet. 'I'll catch up with you next week? There's something I need to do now.' There was no point in learning from experience if those lessons were never used.

Therese nodded. 'Yes. See you then.'

Stella sat at her desk, staring at her tea. She supposed she ought to drink it, but it was beginning to get cold.

She'd wanted to reach out to Rob, but shame and embarrassment had stopped her. She'd been such a fool. She'd known that there was something wrong with Matthew's story and she'd practically invited the situation she'd found herself in. Why hadn't she sat a little further away from him? Why hadn't she just put those darn scissors *down* before she'd mentioned the police…?

The scissors. She could still feel them, hard and cold, pressed against her neck. Not being able to tell whether this was the sharp or the blunt side of the blade, and not quite being able to believe that she had suddenly become one of the stories that came out of A&E from time to time, and there was nothing she could do to stop it.

Trying not to cry or struggle too much, because Matthew's wiry frame was surprisingly strong. Losing herself in Rob's gaze because he was her only way out of this situation. Hearing him say the only words that mattered, again and again, until Matthew heard them.

*'Put the scissors down...let my colleague go.'*

She was going to have to put all of this aside. Get it under control and go and face him. Apologise and hope that they could move on from this. Soon, but not now. Not just yet...

A knock sounded on the door. Phil, probably—he'd been chasing everyone else away and taken it on himself to check on her every now and then. Stella summoned up a smile, hoping it would sound in her voice when she called to him that everything was okay.

Too late. Rob hadn't waited and was already in the room, holding two mugs in one hand and closing the door behind him with the other. He leaned forward, pushing the cold cup of tea to one side and replacing it with one of the cups he'd brought.

'Does this have as much sugar in it as the one Therese made me?' She tried to avoid his gaze, because that reminded her of the stark intimacy that had bound them together so strongly as he'd tried to talk Matthew down.

He leaned forward and took a sip of the cold

tea, grimacing at the taste. 'No. I thought you might like something a bit stronger and not quite as sweet.'

Stella nodded, tasting the hot tea. 'Thanks. That's better. How's Matthew?'

'Medically speaking, he's fine. No one's quite sure how he managed to do what he did, with those injuries and the level of painkillers he had in his system, but he's quiet now and resting under observation. He's in trouble though.'

'I don't want to press charges.' Stella had already decided that.

'That's not going to make any difference. As you know, the hospital has a zero tolerance policy over violence and this took place on their premises. But that's not Matthew's biggest problem. There's another seventeen-year-old in the A&E department at a hospital in Richmond, with the same kinds of wounds that Matthew has, only to his face and leg.'

She was beginning to think a little more clearly now. Rob's strong but not so sweet approach seemed to be working. It felt much more consoling than the blanket assurances that everything was all right and she didn't need to worry.

'Do they have anything to do with each other?'

'Yes. Apparently, there was some kind of dispute between Matthew and this other lad, and they decided to settle it with a fight. The box-cutters were supposed to add a bit of excitement to it all rather than inflicting actual injury, but things went too far and their friends found that it's a bit more difficult to deal with cuts than it is in most action movies. Someone called their parents, which turned out to be the worst move they could have made, because it was them who left the lads at separate A&E departments, hoping they'd be treated and released before anyone worked out the connection.'

'That's…' Incredibly stupid, and at the same time it might just have worked.

'Yeah. I suppose the kids involved have some excuse, but the adults…' He shrugged. 'Apparently, they were trying to keep them out of trouble.'

'What's going to happen to them?'

Rob shook his head. 'I don't know. It's out of our hands now.'

He could speculate, couldn't he? But none of the possibilities that Stella could think of were good ones, and she wasn't sure that she wanted to hear the not so good ones.

'Have some more tea.' Rob's voice was suddenly tender and Stella felt a tear roll down her cheek. Crying in front of him was exactly what she'd been trying to avoid.

But Rob didn't seem to notice. He motioned towards her cup and Stella obediently took a sip. It did make her feel a little better, and she took another.

'Here's what's going to happen—'

'No, Rob. This was my fault. I handled the situation very badly. What's going to happen is that I'm going to apologise and do better next time.' Stella didn't want to hear anything more.

'That's how I feel. I wasn't quick enough and I didn't wrestle him to the ground before he got a chance to put a pair of scissors against your neck. The truth is that we can both find a few things we could have done better, and maybe we're right. Maybe not. We both know that we had to raise the subject of reporting Matthew's injuries to the police, that's part of our job.'

'Perhaps I should have called Terry in…?' That would have been better, now that Stella thought about it.

'Right. Terry's a lovely guy, but having a six-foot-four security guard standing over our patients really isn't the way to go, is it?' Rob leaned forward, looking at her intently. 'This is not an opinion, Stella, it's a fact. What happened was not your fault.'

He didn't sound particularly sympathetic or understanding, but Stella didn't need either of those things. She needed his certainty. His frank opinion and the harsh, consoling reality in his tone.

Stella took another sip of her tea. It felt warm and comforting, and she was feeling stronger now.

'Tackling Matthew to the floor wouldn't have worked, Rob. You did a really good job of defusing the situation and talking him down.'

She saw his hand shake a little as he raised his own cup to his lips. 'Thanks.'

'Are we done now?' Stella hoped that they were. That they could leave this behind them and move forward.

'Not even close. I know exactly what it's like when something happens and you bury it and get on with the job. It works, and so you do it again. And finally, you can't hold all of that grief and pain in one place, and the bubble bursts.'

He was talking about himself. Impassioned by his own memories and the mistakes he felt he'd made. There was no disagreeing with what he said either.

'You're telling me that we need to deal with this?'

'Yes, we do. You've been through a frightening experience, in a situation where your control was taken away from you.' Rob paused, taking a tissue from the box on her desk and handing it to her. Stella hadn't even been aware of her tears, and she rubbed at her face.

It was becoming harder and harder to hold those tears back. She could send Therese and Phil away, tell them that she was okay and just needed a little time on her own, but Rob had been there. She knew that he'd seen her terror, because his steady gaze had reached out to comfort her.

'Phil must have suggested that you go home, because that's what he suggested to me when I saw him on my way in here. So I'm going to call a taxi and take you home. You can change into your pyjamas and eat ice-cream…' He waved his hand in an *or something* gesture.

Stella managed a smile. 'And ice-cream's going to make all the difference, is it?' It had done, in several films that Stella had seen. Generally eaten with your best friend, on a sofa. At least Rob hadn't mentioned calling her best friend, which was a relief because the person she really wanted right now was him.

'Maybe, maybe not. What *is* going to make a difference is that you're going to make an appointment with the hospital counsellor, tomorrow morning. First thing.'

'Am I? Do as I say and not as I do?' Stella wrinkled her nose at him, wondering if telling him to back off was going to work. She very much doubted it, and right now backing off was the last thing that she wanted him to do.

'If you think you're getting your hands on my fruit trees as therapy, you have another think coming. And even though I'm absolutely sure that it's not going to be of any benefit to me, I might learn something I don't know. You might too.'

She puffed out a breath. 'Okay, I will if you will.'

'Good. We'll do it together. Compare notes afterwards.'

Tomorrow seemed like a very long way off at

the moment, and Stella wasn't even sure how she was going to get through the evening.

'You want to get something to eat on the way home? I'm staying at my sister's in Clapham to-night—they're away at the moment but I've got keys to the house. And Emma's looking after Sophie. So I've no train to catch this evening.'

He was being careful. Having somewhere to go for the night ring-fenced their relationship and took all of the uncertainty and stress out of it. Best friends for an evening, but not lovers.

But whatever they chose to call their relationship, Rob was there for her. 'You're not going to give up on me, are you?' She tried to make a joke of it.

'No.' The look in his eyes, and that one word, meant everything.

# CHAPTER SEVEN

ROB HAD GONE into Stella's office with a very clear idea of what he wanted to say, and how he needed to bring his own experience along with him, to convince her that she needed to deal with what had happened before she moved on. Stella could take the truth and, even if he'd sounded a little harsh at times, he'd got through to her. That was really all that mattered.

Even the quiet bustle of the hospital, as they walked down to the taxi rank outside the front entrance, seemed to spook her a little. They'd decided against eating out, in favour of going straight back to her place and getting a takeaway. Stella seemed almost apologetic when she showed him into her third-floor flat. The sitting room was bright in the late afternoon sunshine, and very organised.

'One of these days I might think about getting a few ornaments to dust…' She gave a half-hearted laugh.

'It's overrated. You need a cleaner when you have as much clutter as I do.'

Stella thought for a moment. 'Your place doesn't strike me as cluttered. Unexpected, perhaps. Interesting.'

Rob's house was his refuge. The place he'd run to and made his own, so that he could venture back out again into a life that suited him better. It held all of the pain, as well as the good things, because without one he could never have built the other. Stella's place was different, like a clean sheet of paper. Wherever she kept her doubts and mistakes, it wasn't here.

'I really like your flat. It's calm.' Pale shades, mostly creams with a little blue, took on a new meaning here. There was no story of Stella's life to be discerned from it, just the feeling that now was the best and only time.

She gave him an amused look. 'You mean it doesn't have any personality?'

'There's a lot of space here for *your* personality.' He grinned at her and suddenly their gazes met. The overwhelming feeling that they could be the only two people in the world if they wanted to, had no limits here. No definitions, and none of the things that might keep them apart.

None of the externals, Rob reminded himself. They were still two very different people here, more so perhaps, because there was none of the background noise of everyday life.

He was learning more about her. Her kitchen was as immaculately tidy as the rest of the flat. She liked her curries not too hot, and washed down with the same brand of low-alcohol lager that he did. And when they repaired to the sofa in the sitting room, she didn't automatically turn on the TV and flip through the channels for something to watch. Rob had grown used to his own company during the evening, and it seemed that Stella was too. He wondered whether this might be the time to suggest ice-cream.

'You know…it's days like this that it would be nice to have someone to come home to.' She looked at him, a smile hovering around her lips. 'Thanks for being here, Rob.'

'It's my pleasure. I needed the company too.' Someone to come home to wasn't always what it was cracked up to be. When he'd been married it had more often been someone to rush home to, and then rush back out again for an evening engagement.

'My mum told me something, quite recently.' Stella was clearly still turning the idea over in her head. 'She said that she always knew when Dad had a bad day at work, because he'd come upstairs and just sit by each of our beds for ten minutes. Watching us sleep. I never knew that.'

'I suppose you probably weren't meant to.'

Stella nodded. 'No, I'm sure we weren't. I guess that just being home, with his family, got things back into perspective for him.' She shot him a querying look.

'I wouldn't know. When Kate and I were married, time to stop and take stock didn't feature all that much. That was a large part of the problem.'

He'd spoken more about his feelings to Stella, despite having only known her for a fraction of the time he'd known Kate. That was mostly his fault, but he wondered whether Stella would have let him get away with it, as Kate had.

'You surprise me.' Stella left the thought to hang in the air, not requiring an answer. But Rob wanted to give one.

'Kate and I got married as soon as I left medical school. She knew that I worked long hours, and that was never going to change, but…it was different then. We didn't give much thought to how things would work when we started to want a house in the country, and children. Or when I began to get an increasing number of opportunities at work, and ended up being sucked into all of them. Teaching, researching new techniques… you know.'

'That's what makes you so good at what you do. You just can't leave things alone.' There was a hint of humour in Stella's eyes.

'Yeah. But there's a flip side to it as well. I don't have your focus.'

'You're good at living, though. Sometimes I wonder if there isn't a bit too much clear air around me.'

Rob considered the idea. They were so alike in the challenges they'd chosen to face, and so completely different in the way that they'd solved them. Curiosity was biting chunks out of him and he couldn't resist asking…

'You never thought about getting married?'

'I did, a long time ago. It was a case of wanting too much.'

'I can identify with that.'

Stella's gaze searched his face. She wouldn't find anything new there, because Rob wasn't in the habit of swallowing down what he thought with her.

'My relationships didn't have a very long shelf life when I was studying. I'd go out with someone a few times, they'd say that they were fine with the commitment that a combination of both practical work and study take, and then suddenly they weren't. Then I met someone who didn't seem to mind that I wasn't always around because I was working.'

'It does happen.' Rob was hooked now, and there was no way he could let the subject drop before he'd heard the rest of the story. It seemed to explain all of the little inconsistences that he'd wondered about.

'As my parents have proved. I was thrilled, I thought I'd finally found my Mr Right. And he would have been, if I hadn't minded him taking my evenings at the hospital as carte blanche to go out and spread a little love around. Lust, actually…'

If he'd had Stella for one day in the year, Rob would have lived like a monk for the other three hundred and sixty-four. 'That's... You deserve a great deal more than that, Stella.'

'I thought so too. I never had any regrets about breaking up with him, but I lost the dream. The possibilities, you know?' She smiled suddenly, laying her hand on his arm. 'And my grades went down.'

The sudden contact, even through the thin fabric of his shirt, was electrifying. Rob didn't dare move, in case it deprived him of just one moment of it. 'That's unspeakable.'

'I thought so too. I came to the conclusion that I could do anything I wanted, but not everything. You know what I mean?' She tapped one finger against his arm to emphasise her point, and pure pleasure made him want to laugh out loud.

'Funnily enough, yeah.'

'I decided that the *anything* I wanted was my career. Not so much the career, the surgery. The buzz I get from changing lives.'

He knew what she meant by that as well. Stella took her hand from his arm and it felt as if she'd left a void there, which extended right down to the pit of his stomach.

'And you've never regretted it?'

'No.' She reconsidered for a moment. 'Maybe ninety-nine per cent of the time. Falling to ninety on evenings like this.'

Last week, she'd professed no interest at all in the road not travelled. Tonight, Stella was down to ninety per cent, which left him ten per cent to work with. If he could persuade her differently…

Not tonight. She was vulnerable and far too open to making decisions that she might regret later.

'Do we need ice-cream yet?' He grinned, not finding the change of subject as painful as he'd thought. He wanted, more than anything, to make Stella feel better, more comfortable in her skin after a terrifying experience.

She smiled suddenly. 'I'd say so. Ice-cream would be really nice.'

'You have some in the freezer? Or I'll order in?' He'd seen a takeaway menu for a local ice-cream parlour in the bundle that she'd produced from the kitchen drawer.

'You fancy going out to pick some up, and then bringing it back here to eat on the sofa? I could do with a walk.'

Anything she wanted. And eating it on the sofa made them best friends for the evening. 'Me too.'

They'd dawdled down to the ice-cream parlour, taken their time over their choices, and set up shop on the sofa together to eat it. It was comfortable and companionable, and Rob almost forgot about the unanswered questions that surrounded his and Stella's relationship. Where it might be going, and what it might become. Whether either or both of them could change radically enough to make anything more than a friendship work.

'Do you think that Clapham can do without you for a night? This is a sofa bed.' Stella's spoon rattled in her empty bowl and she tapped the cushion next to her, looking at her watch. It was impossible to tell whether she was saving him a journey or Stella really wanted someone here tonight.

'It'll be hard. But Clapham will manage.' Rob decided that if there was any chance that his presence might make Stella feel more secure and able to sleep, then he'd take it.

He was tired and the sofa bed was comfortable, so sleep came easily after Stella had gone to bed—but every noise woke him. A car accelerating noisily in the street outside. The slight thud of a door banging somewhere in the block of flats. And then the one his sleeping mind had been waiting for. The soft turn of the door handle in the early morning hours.

Then nothing. The doorway was dark, but he could hear her breathing. Short, staccato breaths, which could only mean one thing.

'Hey. You okay?'

'Yes. Sorry to wake you. Go back to sleep.'

No… He wasn't going to let her escape now, not when he could hear the tears that he'd been waiting for all evening in her voice.

'Why don't you come in?'

Silence. Stella was hesitating in the darkness,

and Rob wondered just how far he might go to show her that he was here for her. As far as getting out of bed, or even walking to the doorway? What would happen if she'd already made her way back to her bedroom?

Then he saw her, her footsteps silent on the carpet. Moving into the glow from the streetlights that was filtering in through the curtains. He could see fabric moving around her legs, along with something wrapped around her shoulders, and she seemed smaller somehow. More fragile.

He was reminded of the small form of his niece, trailing her teddy bear and finding her way to his room in the darkness, to tell him that his house made funny noises that frightened her. He'd stayed awake for the rest of the night, guarding little Grace from her fears so that his sister and her husband could get a good night's sleep on a much-needed weekend away. As far as he could see, Stella had no teddy bear with her, but he still felt the same protectiveness. The same feeling that somehow he might keep her from harm.

'You could sit down…?' Preferably not in the chair on the other side of the room, but that was always an option if Stella preferred it.

Her shadow moved towards him and he felt a slight movement as she perched herself right on the far edge of the sofa bed. Still, she was too far away.

'Can we…just talk for a minute?'

'Of course.' Rob eased himself up a little, resting on his elbow. 'What would you like to talk about?'

He saw her shoulders move in a slight shrug. 'I'm not sure.'

'Fair enough. Maybe you could be a little more comfortable while you're thinking about it?'

She hesitated again. And then suddenly she moved, with the kind of certainty that he usually expected from Stella. Sliding onto the bed, she lay down on top of the duvet, next to him. Rob curled his arms around her, pulling the bulk of the quilted bedspread that was wound around her shoulders down a little, so that it would cover her legs and keep her warm.

'That's nice.' She gave him the two words he needed before he could pull her a little closer, curled up against him. He could smell the scent of her hair, feel every breath she took. And then, as if she'd finally found her safe place, Stella began to cry.

'Sorry...' She extricated her hand from the bedspread, wiping her face with her fingers.

'Don't be. This is all okay. It's all good.' Rob caught his breath as he felt Stella's fingers wind around his, clinging on to him as she wept.

# CHAPTER EIGHT

At some point they must have fallen asleep. Rob had woken more than once, and each time Stella was still in his arms, sleeping peacefully. Like a dream that refused to fade. Wanting her the way he did should have kept him awake, but tonight wasn't about that and the gentle rhythm of her breathing lulled him back to sleep again.

Finally, he woke to a loud crash, coming from the kitchen, which was right next door to the sitting room. He sat up in bed rubbing his eyes, and called out to Stella, 'Everything okay?'

Her voice drifted through the open door. 'Yes. Sorry, did I wake you?'

Rob looked at his watch. His brain had got around to processing the noise now, and it had sounded like a pile of baking tins hitting the tiled floor. Either Stella had decided to make cupcakes at seven-thirty in the morning, or this was his wake-up call. Stumbling from the bed and grabbing his clothes, he made for the bathroom.

When he joined her, she was sitting at the table, which was positioned in the window at the far end of the galley of gleaming kitchen units. Opposite her, a place was laid with freshly made toast and coffee.

'Good morning.' Her greeting seemed strangely formal, and Rob detected a hint of morning-after embarrassment. He smiled, sitting down at the table. 'Is toast all right? I haven't got anything else.'

Rob grinned. 'Toast is fine. When I'm working I usually make do with a handful of granola on the way to the car.'

'That's nice with strawberries. Probably a bit messy when you're driving, though...' Stella seemed intent on making conversation.

'Yeah. Not quite as loud as making toast either.'

She stared at him for a moment and then started to laugh. 'I suppose not. I wasn't sure whether you had an alarm clock with you.'

And she hadn't wanted to come back into the sitting room. Fair enough. Last night was...last night. Rob reached for the marmalade to spread some on his toast, and Stella got up to make herself another cup of coffee.

'I suppose...' She was staring fixedly at the machine, clearly avoiding his gaze. 'We don't have to tell a counsellor everything, do we? I mean, about last night.'

'We don't have to tell them anything. Just talk about the things you want to talk about.' It was nice that she didn't want anyone else to know. He didn't either, because it had been special. 'I wasn't going to mention it.'

'No. Neither will I.' She shrugged, picking up her coffee. 'It's not relevant…'

Maybe it was time to cut through all of the uncertainty, and tell her how he really felt. If Stella didn't feel that way then that was okay.

'Last night was one of a kind. It meant a lot to me that you wanted me here. After everything that happened yesterday.'

She smiled suddenly, coming to sit down opposite him. 'It meant a lot to me too, Rob. I couldn't sleep and…'

'Yeah. I know. I needed some company too.'

'Thank you.' Her gaze found his, in that increasingly familiar gesture that acknowledged they'd said all they needed to say.

Maybe things would have been a little less awkward if they'd simply made love last night. They might have cared less and walked away more easily and it would have gone without saying that they'd keep it to themselves. But this had been different, a kind of closeness that had nothing to do with the physical and everything to do with an emotional connection.

'I'll have to see whether the hospital counsellor is free this morning, because I'm operating today.' Stella seemed to have regained her enthusiasm for the day ahead now. Rob knew what a valuable commodity that was. All of the days when he'd woken up, filled with an obscure feeling that the future held more than he could handle, had taught him to cherish these bright mornings.

'Is that an invitation to come and watch you operate?'

She laughed. 'Do you need one, Rob?'

'It's customary.'

'In most circumstances I suppose it is. But my theatre door is always open to you.'

'In that case…what time? I'm interested in seeing what you can do.' Rob knew that was a challenge.

'Maybe *I'm* interested in what you can do.' She responded in just the way he'd thought she might. 'The team meeting's before lunch so that we can start promptly at two o'clock. Don't be late, will you, or I'll have to start without you.'

She couldn't chase his doubts away. She knew that returning was a hard process for him, and that there might be obstacles along the way. But Rob recognised in Stella the approach to the day that he'd once had. That the one and only point of obstacles was that they could be pushed out of the way.

'I'll be there.'

The day had taken a turn for the better. It had started in the very early hours, when Stella had finally decided that lying in bed, allowing her thoughts to prey on her mind, wasn't a good idea. She'd wrenched herself away from the warm duvet, wondering if a glass of water might help. And somehow, she'd found her way to the sitting room door, which wasn't where she was supposed to be going at all.

But she'd been safe in Rob's arms, like a child afraid of the darkness. And that had meant something more than just the practical need to get some sleep before a busy day at work. At the time it had meant everything, and even now Stella couldn't leave it behind. It was like a dream that stubbornly refused to shrivel and die in the morning light.

Phil had already alerted the hospital counsellor, probably deciding that he'd have a battle on his hands in that respect. But when Rob returned from his session, he murmured quietly to Stella to *'Just give it a chance'.* She did, and it helped more than she'd bargained for.

Now the only thing between her and a quiet evening in, followed by an early night, was a student called Ottilie. It was the patient who occupied the place of first importance in an operating theatre, and medical students were usually right at the bottom of the pecking order, considered by many surgeons as beneath their notice. But the two procedures on Stella's schedule this afternoon were straightforward, and she had no concerns about her patients. Ottilie, on the other hand…

She had a lot of potential, and was indisputably bright and enthusiastic. Most students got over their initial nerves in Theatre and settled down, but Ottilie just seemed to get more jittery every time, constantly tripping over her own eagerness to help. She'd managed to get herself in everyone's bad books, which wasn't easy because Stella had a great team, who were generally very supportive of students.

Stella had taken her to one side and explained, as kindly as she could, that the first priority of a student in an operating theatre was to keep out of the way and do as they were told. Ottilie had apologised, promised faithfully to be better in every way in the future, and then the very next time she'd been in Theatre she'd been reduced to tears by a harsh rebuke from the head nurse.

She didn't blame Martin. An operating theatre was a high-pressure environment and it was important to get everything exactly right. And when he was trying to make the first count of all of the instruments, the last thing anyone should do was stand behind him, murmuring their own count, however quietly.

Stella had been forced to ask Ottilie to leave the theatre, and found her crying inconsolably in the locker room afterwards. She'd tried to take a firm but kind stance with her, and explained again how she needed to act in Theatre, but this afternoon was going to be Ottilie's last chance. None of the other surgeons in the department would have her in their operating theatres, and Stella was reluctantly beginning to feel the same way.

Ottilie had attended the team meeting, and as usual she'd taken copious notes. Stella could do nothing but hope for the best, and the way that everyone was ignoring Ottilie wasn't giving her much cause for optimism.

'You want me to keep an eye on Ottilie?' Everyone had filed out of the room, leaving Stella alone with Rob.

'That's not what you're here for, Rob. I've spent a lot of time explaining how she needs to act in Theatre.' Stella bit her lip. 'I don't mean to be ruthless…'

'It's exactly what you should be. It's your job not to allow anything to get in the way of the patient's welfare.' He seemed to understand the dilemma.

'I had a lot of help when I was a student. My dad sat me down and told me exactly what would be expected when I first went into Theatre. He even set up a few practice sessions at home, barking orders at me. I saw quite a different side of him.'

'And now Ottilie's failing and you don't know how to help her? That's not what *you're* here for. I, on the other hand, am a free agent.'

Stella rolled her eyes. 'Believe me, I'm quite aware of that. How on earth did you know about the difficulties with Ottilie, anyway?' He'd been here for just a few days and already he seemed to know what was going on in the unit better than she did.

'There's something to be said for knowing how

everything works, and having the time to just talk to people. I'm quite enjoying it.'

'And something to be said for wanting to prove yourself?' Rob wasn't so very different from Ottilie in that respect, only he had a much better idea of how to go about things.

'That too.' He grinned at her. 'I'm clearly far too transparent.'

Stella gave in. There was no getting over Rob's way of looking at things. 'This is my final offer, then.'

'Make it a good one...'

'I won't ask you to take Ottilie on, because that's not what we invited you here for. If you could point her in the right direction, I'm sure the whole team would be massively relieved, and I'd personally be very grateful.'

Rob made a pretence of thinking about it for a moment. 'Okay, boss. Happy to comply.'

'Do *not* call me boss, Rob! Not when you're busy doing whatever you want...' He was already on his feet, and he didn't turn. But Stella heard him chuckle as he walked out of the room.

If Stella had feared she'd been giving the young woman a hard time, then Rob was outdoing her. She suspected that he'd given Ottilie the task of arranging the theatre shoes carefully on the rack, the named ones at the top and the spares at the bottom, because no one else would have thought to do it. And when she arrived in Theatre, Ottilie was already helping lift the patient onto the operating table, backing away as soon as Rob signalled for her to do so.

So far so good. Stella looked around, checking that everyone was here and ready to start work, and suggested some music.

'Which CD would you like, Ms Parry-Jones?' Ottilie responded.

'What do you think, Sajiv?' Stella turned to the anaesthetist, who generally took charge of the choice of music.

'Number four, Ottilie.' Sajiv shot her a smile. 'Thanks.'

The operation was a delayed breast reconstruction for a woman who'd had a mastectomy six months previously. Stella noticed that Rob had positioned himself and Ottilie in the best vantage point possible, without getting in the way, quietly motioning towards the things she needed to watch. It was actually quite a relief not to have to wonder whether Ottilie was at her elbow, trying to see what she was doing.

'Retractors…' Out of the corner of her eye she saw Ottilie stiffen, clearly knowing that this was a job she could help with, but under Rob's stern gaze she didn't move. 'Rob, can you assist, please?'

He quietly came forward, taking on the job of holding the retractors as if it was the most natural thing in the world for a fully qualified surgeon to do. Ottilie stayed where she was, until Rob motioned for her to come forward and take over from him. When Stella suggested that Rob might like to close for her, he nodded, closing the wound with all the expertise she had come to expect, and giving Ottilie a running commentary on exactly what he was doing. Stella found herself watching as well, in the hope of learning something.

'I think that'll be all right. What do you reckon, Ottilie?'

Ottilie reddened. Even she knew that she wasn't supposed to pass judgement on a surgeon's work, but Rob gave her an encouraging nod.

'Flawless, Mr Franklin.'

'Yep.' Rob knew full well that his work *was* flawless. Stella had come to learn that he expected nothing less of himself. 'Think you can cut the stitches?'

Panic showed in Ottilie's eyes. This was something new, and Stella wondered whether her jumpiness and the way that she crowded everyone was due to lack of confidence. If that was the case, then Rob might be taking a risk here.

He knew that, though. He showed Ottilie exactly what he wanted done, guiding her when she hesitated. They were in danger of running a little late, but Ottilie was turning a corner, learning how to succeed, and despite the team's frustration with her it was what everyone wanted.

When Ottilie was finished, and Rob had nodded

his acceptance of her work, she stood back. The team took over, an efficient machine that worked with Rob to finish on time. Stella thanked everyone, and then turned to Ottilie.

'You did well this afternoon.'

Ottilie beamed at her. 'Thank you, Ms Parry-Jones. I really appreciate your having me here.'

'Scrub out…' Rob jerked his thumb towards the swing doors leading out of the operating theatre, and Ottilie nodded, hurrying away.

'What on earth have you done to the poor girl?' Stella frowned up at him.

'I collared her and took her for lunch—we had sandwiches in the park. She had a few very interesting things to say for herself.' Rob shot her an enigmatic look and it was clear that Stella was going to have to ask if she wanted to know more.

'You're going to tell me? Or do I have to force it out of you?'

'Well, if you must know…and I'm a little upset over having to give up my people management secrets…' He grinned at her, clearly not upset at all. 'Ottilie's the first person in her family ever to go to university, let alone medical school. When she told her parents that she was going to start on a surgical training module they threw a party, telling the whole family that their daughter was going to be a surgeon.'

'Ah. The weight of expectation.'

'Yes. She's got all she needs to succeed, but she's

just terrified she'll let everyone down, and that's pushing her into making mistakes. So I told her that there was only one person that she needed to impress.'

Stella folded her arms, shifting from one foot to the other, to ease the ache in her back. 'The only person she needed to impress was you, I suppose?'

'I can give her immediate feedback. Everyone else is too busy to notice that she tidied the shoe rack.'

'And classifying according to job descriptions. I did wonder who'd done that.'

'Exactly my point, Stella. Your concentration is rightly on the patient, and you don't have the time to discuss shoe racks with student doctors. I asked her to do it, she did it really well and I told her she'd done a good job.'

Stella puffed out a breath. 'So I'm the big bad wolf in all of this.' Rob opened his mouth, obviously about to deny it and she held up her hand. '*You* didn't say that. I'm saying it.'

'If you were, I'd have had my head bitten off before now. You focus on what you need to focus on, and that's what makes you a good surgeon. That doesn't put you in the wrong, you just have a different job description.'

Stella had always felt that way, but it was good to hear someone say it. Good to hear *Rob* say it, actually.

'Do you miss it?'

Rob shrugged. 'Not in the slightest. That tingling feeling I got when I stepped into the theatre is probably just my blood pressure. I ought to get that sorted.'

'I can take your blood pressure if you want me to.' She called his bluff and Rob shook his head. 'I'm thinking of coming in on Saturday to work up a plan for Anna's surgery. I meant to start on that yesterday but never managed to get that far. If you're around…?'

'I'd love to join you. But I need to be back at home. I'm on call.'

Right, then. Stella could suggest an alternative, or let it slide. Rob needed his weekends, probably more than ever since he'd started to step back into a life that had once almost broken him. But he did look genuinely disappointed.

'I could always drive down to yours. If you want me to, that is—it's probably better just to email you with my thoughts and we could discuss it next week.'

'The train's faster.' He smiled suddenly. 'I'll pick you up at the station if you text me and let me know when you're arriving…'

Had it really been just a couple of weeks? Rob felt as if he'd experienced one of those major turning points in life, where one moment could change everything.

That had never happened before. Change had

always felt like a gradual process, which relied on a myriad different things. But his life felt as if it had been chopped in two—before Stella and after Stella.

It probably wasn't Stella at all. His lingering discontent with a life that didn't include the thing he'd worked so hard to achieve, the excitement at the thought of stepping into an operating theatre again…. That *had* to be it.

All the same, when he drew up at the station on Saturday morning and saw Stella waiting outside, sunglasses perched on the top of her head and wearing a sleeveless blouse with a summer skirt and flat sandals, surgery was the last thing on his mind. His world tipped, much as it had when he'd first seen her, but this time the reaction was far more dizzying.

He'd set up a table and chairs in the shade of a spreading oak tree that had been standing since before the house was built. The breeze tugged at her skirt, its fingers riffling through her hair as they worked, and when it was time for lunch he brought lemonade, sandwiches and a bowl of cherries from the kitchen. Finally, Stella sat back in her seat.

'I think…we're almost there.'

'Yep. We can run through a few simulations next week, to settle our outstanding points.' They'd disagreed over a couple of suggestions that Rob had made, both impassioned and neither willing to back down because the stakes were so high. Rob had fought for his ideas before, but it had never felt quite so delicious.

Surgery was one thing, both challenging and rewarding in equal measure, and even though it had broken him he still loved it. But Stella was quite another. She understood him and she could meet needs that he'd never even realised he had. And that all-important but indefinable thrill whenever he saw her was there too. It was just too bad that their differing lifestyles meant that they could never be happy together.

# CHAPTER NINE

THE WEEKS LEADING up to Anna's surgery were busy. Rob had immersed himself in the work of the unit, and always seemed to have a student or one of the junior doctors with him, taking copious notes of everything he said. They ran simulations, explored possibilities and did the practical work of making sure that the long surgery would be done in such a way that Rob could take over from Stella at regular intervals, to give her a chance to rest. The prosthetics they'd need to reshape Anna's shattered jaw had been made, and they were ready. Stella was excited about the possibilities and aware of everything that might go wrong in equal measure.

She and Rob faced each other across the operating table. The gallery above their heads was full, students and junior doctors pressed tightly together. Around them, the team that Stella had chosen, who had worked together for long enough to be able to anticipate most of her requests before she even voiced them. Anna had been prepped and anesthetised, and now everyone's attention was directed on them. Stella's was directed on Rob.

All she could see was his eyes, but that was

enough. It was ten in the morning, and the surgery was expected to run through the whole day, and probably into the late evening. But they'd be there for each other. There for Anna, and striving for the new life that she wanted.

'Sajiv...?' She didn't need to ask for the music, she knew that Sajiv would have prepared something.

'Coming right up.' The quiet strains of an orchestra threaded through the air of anticipation. Sajiv generally started with a classical piece, moving on to something a little more modern later.

Stella felt for the exact point to start her first incision. She saw Rob's nod and took a breath, feeling the theatre nurse place the scalpel in her hand...

As soon as they'd started, all of the hopes and fears dissolved. There was just the present, and the intense concentration needed for the task at hand. One of the screens above their heads displayed their progress through the complex set of procedures, mostly for the benefit of the gallery because she and Rob been over it so many times that it was fixed very firmly in Stella's head. Every time she stepped back to stretch or check on the live X-ray screen, Rob was there, almost a part of herself who knew everything she knew, saw everything she saw.

By midday, the work on the scar on Anna's forehead had been completed and Stella took a break. A visit to the ladies' room, which she didn't really need but there was a long afternoon ahead of her. Something to eat and drink, which wasn't completely necessary either, but when they'd discussed the plan, Rob had reminded her of the need to pace herself.

By two o'clock they were ahead of schedule. At three they had to stop until Sajiv was happy that Anna's vital signs were steady again. At five, Stella stepped back from the table for a moment and realised that her back and shoulders were beyond aching.

'Take a break?' Rob murmured the words and she nodded. They weren't finished yet, but it had already been a long day and it was necessary to keep physical and mental tiredness at bay.

'Yes.' He would take over her role while she stretched her complaining muscles.

At seven o' clock in the evening came the words that everyone had been waiting for. Stella glanced around at the team, and then at Rob, who nodded his agreement to her unspoken question. The demanding and intricate work of reshaping Anna's jaw had been done, and they were ready for the next part of the procedure.

'We'll close now.'

She didn't need to tell anyone what to do. Rob was ready to take on the next part of the process, and the theatre nurse was already counting the instruments and the large pile of discarded swabs. Now wasn't the time to lose her concentration, but she could step back a little, taking on a support role in the intricate task of moving the skin flap on Anna's neck upwards and applying skin grafts where needed, ready for the wounds to be dressed and for healing to begin.

They were done just before midnight. The team who would care for Anna as she regained consciousness swung into action, and Stella stepped back from the table for the last time.

'Thanks, everyone. You all rock…' Finally, she had a moment to glance up at the gallery and she was surprised to see many of the faces who'd been there this morning. Phil Chamberlain was on his feet, and the silent applause from the gallery was mirrored in the operating theatre below, a short burst of quiet clapping that didn't often happen, but meant a great deal when it did.

'*You're the one who rocks…*'

As they scrubbed out together, Rob murmured the words and even though she was suddenly far too tired to be feeling anything, tingles ran the whole length of Stella's aching spine.

'Not so bad yourself.' She grinned at him. Stella was far too tired for grinning as well, it felt as if her face was about to tear apart under the strain.

They both knew the first thing that they had to do now. Rob bumped his arm against her shoulder in an expression of support as they walked through to the lounge, where Jess was waiting with Anna's parents. The hospital's patient support team would have told them that there would be no news during the course of the day, but all the same it looked as if they'd been here for a while, filling up the bins with coffee cups. Stella walked over to where they were sitting and waited a few moments until they were ready to hear her news.

'Jess, Mr and Mrs Leigh… I'm very pleased to tell you that Anna's surgery has gone as well as we'd hoped. She's in Recovery now, and they'll take her through to Intensive Care for the night, and probably most of tomorrow. But as soon as she's back on the ward, you'll be able to see her.'

'She's going to be all right?' Mrs Leigh asked tremulously, clutching her husband's hand.

'It's too early to give you a complete response. Anna still has a long road ahead of her.' Rob smiled encouragingly. 'But she's come through the surgery well, which is very promising, and we have reason to feel optimistic.'

Mrs Leigh burst into tears, and her husband hugged her. Jess jumped to her feet, enveloping Stella in a bear hug. That was the last thing she needed at the moment, but she didn't have the heart to pull away.

'Thank you. Thank you so much…'

'If you want to thank her, then not hugging would be a great idea.' Rob's voice sounded full of humour and understanding. Jess let her go suddenly.

'Sorry… You must be exhausted.' Exhaustion didn't really cover it, but Stella smiled, nodding. 'Thank you for everything…' Jess seemed to be looking around for someone else to hug, but made do with grabbing Rob's hand and shaking it.

'Why don't you go home and try to get some sleep? You won't be able to see her tonight, but I promise you that Anna's in very good hands and that she's being well cared for,' Stella suggested and Jess shook her head.

'I just… I know it's crazy but I just feel that I want to stay as close as I can…' Jess pursed her lips. 'They will tell me, won't they? How she's doing?'

'Yes, they will. You're Anna's partner and she signed a form, nominating you and her parents as her joint next of kin. You have a right to ask and be answered.' That hadn't always been the case and, after a day spent waiting around with nothing to do but worry, Jess had probably forgotten that this had all been dealt with.

'Then…' Jess turned to Anna's parents. 'Why don't you both go home and get some sleep? I can catch some shut-eye on the couch here, and I promise I'll call you straight away with anything.'

Jess was clearly determined to stay, and Mrs and Mrs Leigh both looked very tired.

'That's a good idea.' Rob turned to Anna's parents. 'There's nothing you can do here, and the best thing you can do for Anna now is to pace yourselves and be ready for when she wakes up. She's going to need you then.'

'He's right, Jo.' Mr Leigh squeezed his wife's hand. 'Why don't you come with us, Jess? You don't want to be here all on your own.'

Jess shook her head miserably.

'We'll get someone to find Jess a bed in one of the family rooms. She can get some sleep, and she'll be woken if there's any news to pass on to you,' Rob suggested.

'That sounds great, thank you.' Jess smiled at him, clearly beginning to feel that she might be able to sleep now. In an effort to stay on her own feet, Stella reminded herself that this fatigue was a good thing, a result of her allowing herself to relax because things were going well.

Handshakes were exchanged, and there were more thank-yous than Stella could register. She followed Rob out of the waiting room and into the corridor, too weary to take much notice of anything until Rob stopped suddenly.

'Ottilie!'

Stella turned to see Ottilie, standing behind the open door of the waiting room. It had concealed her presence while they were talking to Anna's family, and Ottilie was pressing her body against the wall now, clearly hoping that it might open up and swallow her.

'Sorry…' Ottilie backed away, clearly hoping to make her escape in the opposite direction, but Rob called her back.

'Anything we need to know?' Rob fixed her with a look that seemed designed to break down anyone's defences. Stella certainly couldn't resist it.

'Sorry. No. I wanted to see how you handled this part…' She turned to Stella. 'I was watching whenever I had some free time today. I think you're amazing.'

'And very tired,' Rob chided her gently. 'Are you thinking about how much you have ahead of you?'

He'd got it exactly right and Ottilie reddened. 'I don't think I'll ever be able to do what you do, Ms Parry-Jones.'

'You may not be able to do it now, and you probably can't see far enough ahead to believe you'll ever make it. You'll just have to take it from me that you're going in the right direction, even if you do feel that you're travelling blind.'

Ottilie nodded. Rob had clearly said something of the sort to her before, and was reinforcing that message.

'Go home, and get some sleep. If you want to follow up on this patient then you can do it tomorrow, and you can leave your write-up of all your observations in my pigeonhole. I look forward to reading it.' Rob's tone was firm but kindly, and Ottilie looked up at him with thinly disguised hero-worship.

'Thank you. I'm on it…' Ottilie turned and hurried away, and Rob called after her.

'Sleep first.'

'You think she knows she's headed for the medical imaging suite?' Stella murmured to him.

'Probably not. She might wait around the corner until the coast's clear to come back this way again.' Rob chuckled. 'She's worth the effort, you know. I think she'll make a great surgeon if she just stops worrying about the future and concentrates on the present. I've been looking through some of the write-ups she's done on the surgeries she's attended and she's good.'

'You've been helping her?'

'Yeah. I think she's got a lot of potential, and that she's just going through a bit of a rough patch. Once she stops thinking about whether she's doing the right thing or not, she's surprisingly thoughtful and assured. She's very bright, and she was used to being the best kid in the class at school. Then she came to university and found herself among a load of other bright and ambitious young people. It takes a bit of getting used to.'

'And you know this how?' Perhaps Rob had taken a course in psychology in his spare time, during the last three years.

'I live in a village. Seven hundred and ninety-nine people…in a few days we're expecting it to be a round eight hundred. And I'm a GP, remember? When they're awake, patients have a habit of telling you things.' Rob smiled down at her. 'Ottilie's quite right, of course. You *are* amazing.'

Stella nudged his arm with her elbow. 'Don't underestimate your own part in this.'

A night spent curled up in his arms had brought them closer, and today had brought them closer still. In different ways, perhaps, but it all came down to trust. The kind of trust that had made her feel safe when every shadow held a young lad with a pair of scissors in his hand was the same kind of trust that allowed her to move back from a patient, knowing that she was leaving them in good hands. It had helped Rob and Stella to work together seamlessly, and give Anna their best.

If she took his arm, held on to him as tightly as she wanted to, she was sure that Rob would respond. But the thought that Ottilie might decide that the medical imaging suite wasn't on the way to anywhere that she wanted to go and suddenly appear behind them made Stella think better of the idea. She'd seen enough in Rob's eyes today to know that if she touched him now she wouldn't let him go.

'Are you going to get some sleep yourself, now?' His raised eyebrow told Stella that he knew full well she wouldn't.

'I may go and shut my eyes for ten minutes in my office. I want to be around to see Anna get settled in the ICU. How about you? You're not going back to Sussex at this time of night, are you?'

'No, I've taken myself off the on-call rota for the weekend. I thought that I'd stick around for a little while too, and then go back to my sister's place and tip myself onto the couch in an effort not to wake anyone.'

'There's always Phil's office couch, he won't mind if you crash out on it for a couple of hours.' If curling up with him on the smaller couch in her office was out of the question, at least they'd be in the same building.

'Sounds blissful.' He stopped outside the lifts, stabbing at the call button with his finger, and the doors to one of the cars opened obligingly.

They were alone in the lift for probably less than a minute. But it felt a great deal longer, because Rob was a man who made good use of his time. Catching her hand in his, he raised it to within an inch of his lips, his eyes suddenly dark and searching. When Stella gave a small nod, he planted a kiss on her fingers.

'Rob, I...' Too late. The lift doors were opening and they were back in a world where, even at this hour, there would be someone around to see whatever passed between them.

And now anything that did pass between them would be all about loss and regret. They'd see each other again—there was still a lot left to do for Anna—and Rob had become so much a part of the department now that he had a lot of loose ends to tie up before he could leave. But they wouldn't be battling together, against each other and against all the odds. They'd changed each other's lives and now everything was going to be focused on moving on.

'I know…'

Of course he did; he'd been there too. It was almost a relief not to have to put it into words, because there was nothing that Stella could say which would reflect the way she felt.

# CHAPTER TEN

ROB HAD STAYED in London until Sunday afternoon, catching a few hours' sleep on Friday night, before going with Stella to see how Anna was early the following morning. He'd gone to his sister's house on Saturday evening, knowing that it was a very poor idea to take Stella up on the offer of her sofa bed for the night. It wasn't very likely that he would stay in his bed, and Stella in hers, after the closeness of the last couple of days.

Before he left the hospital on Sunday afternoon, ready to get a good night's sleep before going to work on Monday morning, there were a few moments for a goodbye. Only that goodbye had already been said, in unplanned, stolen moments in a lift. He'd already felt the loss, and it seemed as if they were just going through the motions.

'I'll see you.' She smiled up at him.

'Yeah. Around.' He grinned back at her.

'Around where?' Stella did like to keep things as predictable as possible and in a sudden urge to see whether she might compromise with him, he decided not to set a date.

'I know where you are. You know where I am. Probably at a time when we least expect it.'

'You mean I'm not going to get the chance to prepare for it?'

'Absolutely not. Just take my word that it'll happen…'

As the week wore on Rob became more annoyed with himself, as he didn't like making empty promises. He'd given his word to Stella in the heat of the moment, and it had seemed the right thing to say at the time, but with each day that passed it felt more and more like a mistake. Stella was beautiful, perfect just as she was, but he'd let a lot of people down—Kate, his colleagues at the hospital… Rob might be determined not to do the same to Stella, but he had a lot of previous in that respect.

And they were so very different. He loved the country, the slow pace of a small village where he knew each of his patients personally and was liable to bump into any one of them whenever he went to buy a paper or post a letter. Stella thrived on the fast pace and pressures of surgery in the heart of the city. He might miss that, but Rob wasn't sure how he could ever make it his whole life again.

She'd promised to email him with news of Anna, and Stella had kept her word. Short intimate messages, which really should have had kisses at the bottom but didn't. He'd replied in kind, alluding to the photographs and reports that she'd enclosed, and wondering whether this was the beginning of the end. Whether Stella had realised that it would be hard to maintain a relationship in the present, when neither of them had any clear idea of what they wanted for the future, and was letting him down gently.

He spent Thursday and Friday digging a ditch. It wasn't an entirely necessary ditch, more a precaution against unusually heavy rain in the autumn, but the repetitive, tiring nature of the work helped him to keep his mind away from what-ifs. By Saturday, the trench was a lot longer and deeper than any stretch of the imagination required, and he resorted to weeding the kitchen garden.

When he heard a car drawing up outside the house he didn't take off his muddy boots to go inside and answer the door. Whoever it was would know that he'd probably be working in the garden. Parcels would be left on the doorstep and visitors would come and find him. He heard footsteps on the path around the house and something about them made him turn suddenly.

Stella. Dressed in jeans and a brightly coloured summer top, and looking as delicious as a long, cool glass of lemonade. His mouth suddenly felt very dry.

'To what do I owe this pleasure?' Rob managed to summon up the words, and add a smile to them.

'Not expecting me?'

He hadn't expected this. Stella was his dream of a woman, but the way she looked right now was beyond even his wildest dreams. He couldn't see any difference from the way she usually looked, although he always liked her more casual weekend outfits better than her monochrome work attire. Maybe it was a week spent wondering whether he'd ever see her again that made her red hair seem so fiery in the sunshine.

'If I had been I'd have answered the door. And planted up hanging baskets to welcome you.'

'That would have been very nice. If I'd heard you were up in town on one of your days off, and could drop round for dinner, I'd have gone for flaming torches on my doorstep...'

Stella's taste for the dramatic. There was no question about it now. She'd taken the next step, and he'd responded. They would be seeing things through, wherever it led them. Not yet, though, because she'd opened the leather bag that was tucked under her arm, and taken out an envelope. She held it out towards him, and Rob caught sight of the hospital's logo in one corner.

'What's this?'

'It's something that Phil came up with. I agreed that it was a great idea, and said that I'd bring his proposal down to you at the weekend.'

Rob took off his gardening gloves and dropped them onto the ground. Luckily, his oldest jeans and shirts were in the wash, after having come in close contact with the ditch, and he had a relatively respectable shirt on today. Without the gloves, he looked relatively clean and tidy—other than his boots, which were still on his feet and caked with soil.

He opened the envelope and drew out a wad of paper, skimming the letter from Phil, which was paperclipped to a larger document underneath. 'He wants me to *what*...?'

'It's... I don't know what you'd call it. Staff development in partnership with the teaching arm of the hospital. Mentoring, maybe. You have a lot of skills and knowledge, and you have a way of thinking around things that...' Stella shrugged. 'It's only for a day a week, and perhaps some work from home via email or video-conferencing. But you might enjoy it.'

Rob smiled. He could see which way this was going. 'And it might tempt me to come back? Because I'm wasting all my valuable training, working here as a GP?' The idea hurt, because he knew he'd disappointed everyone—the people who'd supported him in his career, and the teachers who'd inspired him.

'No... Well, yes. I'll admit that I think it's a waste that you have so much skill and talent and you're not using it. But I understand now why you had to stop, because it was eating you up. I told Phil that he shouldn't expect you to come back full-time unless you were absolutely ready, because if this isn't right for you then *that's* the real waste. It's your decision, and I'm not here to persuade you either way.'

'It's tempting. I'll admit that.' Stella's honesty had made it even more tempting. 'One thing, though. Is my email suddenly not working?'

Her smile told him that there was nothing wrong with his email. 'I don't know. You'd be a better judge of that than I am.'

That was all he needed to hear. And now there was no going back. He took one step forward, his shadow falling across her face. He was already lost in her gaze when she reached up, putting her arms around his neck.

It was one hell of a kiss. The kind of kiss that might bring him to his knees if it lasted too long, but which made him feel stronger than he had in a long while. She was soft and sweet-smelling in his arms, and yet Stella was strong enough to kick down the barriers that lay between them.

'I never thought it would be *this* nice.' Stella's lips seemed redder, her eyes brighter.

'You underestimated me?' Rob raised an eyebrow.

'No. It seems that my imagination's not as good as I thought it was.' She moved against him, kissing him again. One more unimaginably beautiful kiss.

'Maybe we should go inside. Talk…' Rob knew exactly where this was leading and he couldn't stop it. But he wanted Stella to be sure.

'I think that's a very good idea.'

* * *

This was all that Stella had dreamed about but hadn't dared to hope for. She knew that she and Rob were friends, and that they had a connection, but that didn't mean that they should be lovers. For the first time in her life, she was going into a relationship without knowing where it would lead, and she was actually okay with that. Okay with the idea that Rob had the power to turn her life upside down, because she trusted him enough to know that he wouldn't.

He stepped out of his boots and into the kitchen before quickly making for the sink and soaping his hands, automatically beginning to clean each finger in a process that would take another ten minutes to complete.

'You're taking time to think about this?' Stella wound her arms around his waist, laying her head on his back.

'I want you to be sure.' He abandoned the scrubbing and turned the tap off, twisting around to face her. 'Really sure. Because I don't know how this is going to work out.'

'That's my line, isn't it? Always wanting to predict the end before I commit to the beginning. Perhaps I'll just steal yours, and tell you that I want this beginning. And that I trust you enough to take it without knowing the end.'

His face darkened suddenly. 'I'm not entirely convinced that you should trust me…'

She picked up the towel by the sink, carefully drying his hands. In the heat of his gaze, even that small intimacy felt a lot like foreplay. 'Too late, Rob. There's nothing you can do about that.'

She kissed his lips, feeling his arms gently embracing her. This was just delicious. There was passion there, she could feel it in the tension of his body, but Rob was clearly determined not to rush.

'How are we going to take this?' His kisses trailed across her jawline, towards her ear.

'Any way you want it…'

She felt the pressure of his touch reduce suddenly. She liked the way he hesitated. It showed that he understood the challenge she'd just thrown him.

'Sorry to interrupt the moment. But you're going to have to explain exactly what you mean by that.'

'I know what I like. Finding out what you like might add a few things to that list.'

He got it now. She wasn't inviting him to take, she wanted him to give. And his body supplied the answer she wanted, clearly aroused at the thought.

'And of course you're more than capable of telling me to stop if my fantasies don't happen to coincide with yours.'

Oh! Fantasies! Rob really *did* know how to do this, perhaps better than she did. The thought of getting acquainted with all of his fantasies, and being able to show him hers, was beyond allure.

Beyond the sharp pull of arousal, and moving into something that was deeper and wilder.

'In a hot minute.'

'Make that thirty seconds…' His smile made her tremble, because suddenly Stella had no idea what Rob was going to do next.

He backed her against the worktop, lifting her up onto it. She tugged at his shirt and he let her pull it over his head, but when her fingers went for the waistband of his jeans he brushed them away, pushing her knees apart so that he could stand close and pull her against him. She felt his arm around her, supporting her back, his other hand caressing her neck. Suddenly Stella knew exactly what he wanted. He wanted to bring her to fever pitch, and he wanted to do it slowly.

She wound her arms around his neck, feeling the warmth of his skin under her fingers. The smooth contours of bone and muscle. His scent. One by one, he was slowly undoing the small buttons on her blouse, and it was driving her crazy.

'Look at me.' There was no hint of command in his voice, but when she met his gaze she was caught, unable to get away. He planted soft kisses onto her lips as he slowly eased her out of her blouse, and she shivered at the touch of his fingers on her skin.

'You…' He'd found the thin, silky material of her bra and she gasped at the caress of his fingers. 'You could…'

'Take it off? Yeah, I could. Now or later?'

He made *later* seem like a sensual delight that was worth waiting for and really didn't need to be hurried. 'Later's good.'

His fingers skimmed her breast and Rob's mouth curved in a smile when she gasped. Gently gripping her arms, he pushed her hands behind her, winding his fingers loosely around her wrists. His light grip would have allowed her to escape in a second. He wanted her to stay put of her own volition and wait to find out what he was going to do. The thought made her shiver with desire.

Rob kissed her shoulders, running the fingers of his free hand lightly along the lacy edging of her bra. Touching, kissing her skin, everywhere but where she really wanted him to go. She pressed her lips together, determined not to beg, trembling at his every touch. Rob seemed intent on watching, enjoying every part of the arousal that was running through her body. *Later* had been a very good decision...

By the time they'd got upstairs and finished stripping off their clothes, Stella was so lost in him that she could barely notice anything else. Still he couldn't be persuaded to rush. He pressed a condom from the drawer of the bedside cabinet into her hand. It was there for her to use any time she wanted, and Stella wondered just how long she'd be able to hold out.

Minutes, hours—this was too all-consuming to even register the passing of time. They were both so aroused that it seemed impossible that they could wait any longer, but this slow dance was so exquisite that it always seemed to hold a few minutes more of enjoyment.

'Rob…' Finally, she grabbed his hand, moving it down between her legs, feeling his fingers caress her most sensitive places.

'Like this?' He trailed kisses across her breasts.

'Yes! Yes, just like that…' The orgasm hit her like a bolt of lightning, tearing its way through her. Rob stayed with her, making sure that it lasted, and then gently bringing her back down again. He knew just what to do, and had a rare talent for keeping the momentum going without forcing the pace too much.

'How do you know how to do that?' Stella smiled at him lazily, feeling her desire for him retreat and then slowly start to build again, like the insistent rise and fall of an incoming tide.

'You give yourself away.' He brushed his lips against the spot where a pulse beat in her neck. Then he slid his fingers gently back inside her, pressing in just the right spot to make her gasp. 'You're so generous in your reactions.'

And Rob was a man who took enough care to watch for those reactions. She pressed the condom into his hand. 'Now you have to give something of yours to me.'

He smiled, leaning away from her for a moment to roll the condom into place. When he eased inside her she could feel that their long foreplay had been just as stimulating for him as it had for her. He moved slowly at first, finding out how their bodies worked together and what gave them both the most pleasure.

'Rob!' Stella choked out his name as he slid one hand beneath her hips, lifting them a little so that he could go deeper. His eyes darkened and his sudden, sharp gasp told her that they'd just got it exactly right.

And then it got better. She could feel his body, burning up against hers, his movements more and more assertive as blind passion began to take hold. Stella squeezed the muscles that cradled him, and a low groan escaped his lips. Once more and her own orgasm came hard and fast, her body arching beneath his to savour every moment of it. Then Rob let out a cry and she held him tight as his body stiffened and convulsed.

There were no words for this. He cradled her in his arms and she felt her heart beating wildly against his. Slowly, their bodies started to wind back down again, and he rolled away from her for a moment before curling his limbs around hers.

'Are you...all right?' It felt as if they'd both spun together into a different world, one where they might have to tread carefully for a while. But Rob's low chuckle reassured her.

'I've been way better than just *all right* for a while. I think I've reached a completely different plane now. You?'

'You took me right there with you, Rob.'

Rob had thought about what being with Stella might be like, but his imagination couldn't possibly have stretched to anything like this. She liked the same things that he did. Instead of snuggling together under the covers and letting their bodies relax into sleep, she wanted to continue their voyage of exploration. Now it was relaxed and contemplative, her fingers gently tracing the route of all the primary muscles in his shoulders and arms, where previously she'd gripped them so tight that he was sure there must be some evidence on his skin. He liked that too. That she hadn't left him exactly as she'd found him.

He'd expected that she would be bold, because that was how Stella was in everything else. But he hadn't expected quite this kind of assertiveness. It had challenged him to take charge because she had to know how much he wanted to please her. It had left him in no doubt that he *had* pleased her.

When the warmth of their bodies had started to cool, he'd risen from the bed, taking her on his lap in the large wicker chair that stood by the window and wrapping them round with the quilt that hung across its back.

'Do I get to call you *boss* now?' He kissed her forehead.

'Only here. And only if I get to call you boss too...'

Rob chuckled. 'You have a deal.'

She looked up at him questioningly. 'Do I? Is there any time limit on that?'

One of them was bound to say it, sooner or later. Was there a way forward for them?

'Sussex isn't so far from London. Neither of us is going to have to move house.'

Stella moved against him, planting a kiss on his cheek. 'Moving house would be easy.'

They'd tumbled into this, driven only by the certain knowledge that they wanted to be together. And now reality was beginning to bite.

'We've done this before. Started something and agreed to find out where it leads. We have different lives, different aims, but there's no reason why we can't travel together and see where it takes us.'

'I'd like that...' Stella hesitated. Something was on her mind, and Rob could guess what it was.

'If you're not here, that doesn't mean that I'm not still committed to you, Stella. That's non-negotiable.' He'd never treat her the way she'd been treated in the past.

She smiled suddenly, her gaze searching his face. 'For someone who's afraid of messing up, you make a very good job of *not* messing up.'

'That's good to know.' He kissed her to seal the deal. 'Whatever comes next...'

'We'll handle it. Let's concentrate on today now, eh?'

Rob had thought that Stella had given him everything, but now there was more. They'd found a tomorrow that they could both live with, and that meant they truly had today. They could trade fantasies—there was none of the tentative worry that something might shock, because he knew that Stella was capable of a simple *yes* or *no*. Right now, he could believe that she was capable of anything that she set her mind on doing, and the thought that she'd set her mind on him was the ultimate turn-on.

'You like to watch, don't you?' She planted a kiss on his cheek. 'I like you watching me.'

That was sorted, then. One more thing to look forward to. 'Don't stop there.'

'I notice that you have a mirror over there...' She freed one hand from the folds of the quilt, pointing towards the antique cheval mirror that stood in the corner of the room. It didn't get much use, but it had caught Rob's eye and he'd bought it at a local auction and cleaned the wooden frame.

'Which can be moved to the location of your choice.'

'I noticed that too. Or we could always swap places.'

The thought of watching Stella climb on top of him, and what she might do with him when she did, was almost too much to bear. She smiled, moving gently against him, which only made it more difficult to resist gathering her up right now and taking her back to the bed.

'So soon?' she teased him.

'It's been hours. Are you telling me that you're done with me already?'

'Not a chance.' Her fingers brushed against his erection, and Rob caught his breath. 'Impressive.'

'Really? You know all the right things to say to a guy. Or are you just very easy to please?' It was the first time that anyone had chosen to describe him as impressive, and maybe that was because this was the first time that Rob had let himself simply go with the flow, unhampered by his own expectations and goals.

'I'm only speaking as I find.' She kissed him, her mouth sweet and inviting. When he cupped her breast with his hand, Stella looked up at him, her eyes full of desire.

'How are we going to take this…?' The mischievous glint in her eyes told him that she wanted to turn the tables on him now.

'Any way you want it, sweetheart…'

# CHAPTER ELEVEN

THEY'D BEEN MAKING love for a good part of the morning and most of the afternoon. Stella could have stayed here all evening as well, but they had to eat.

Rob had chuckled when she'd asked him for a hanger so that she could fold her clothes neatly over it in the bathroom, where the mist from the shower would deal with the creases. She'd defiantly snatched up the shirt he'd been wearing and put it on, hoping that he wouldn't take another clean one from the closet, because a physique like Rob's could stand a little more inspection and she wasn't quite ready to leave the hours they'd spent together behind. He'd pulled on his jeans and a T-shirt, which was a good enough compromise since she could still trace every muscle through the thin fabric. They'd padded barefoot down to the kitchen to raid the fridge.

'Shall I put a couple of these part-cooked baguettes into the oven?' Stella inspected the packaging.

'Yeah, good idea. There's ham and cheese in there somewhere to go with them...'

'*Somewhere*' was about right. Stella began to

sort the contents of his fridge into some kind of order and he looked up from the papers she'd brought this morning, which had caught his attention almost as soon as they'd entered the kitchen.

'Hey! Don't mess up my system!'

'There's a system?' She frowned at him.

'Yeah. I buy a load of stuff and I put it into the fridge on the right-hand side. Then what I don't eat gets pushed to the left the next time I go shopping.'

'Okay.' Stella inspected some of the sell-by dates, which backed up his claim. 'Sorry. I see how it works now. Get on with your reading.'

'Tidy up a bit if you absolutely have to, as long as you keep the right/left thing going.' He grinned at her and started to read again, his finger poised beneath each line to focus his concentration. Stella decided that since he'd opened the door to the idea, he could hardly object if she threw away the half carton of milk hidden at the back on the left. There was a full carton on the right, and she'd use that one for their coffee.

She took a quiche from the left-hand side of the fridge, along with ham and cheese and all of the salad items she could find, putting them on the table. By the time the oven had heated and the bread was ready, Rob had finished reading and was ready to eat.

'You know that it's not going to stay like that, don't you?' He nodded towards the closed door of the fridge.

'Yes, I know. You'll have to ask me back some time, so I can do it again.'

His gaze suddenly held all of the warmth of their time together upstairs. 'Any time you like. My fridge door is always open to you.'

They ate in silence for a while, their makeshift meal seeming like a feast because, however messy Rob's fridge was, he clearly bought local produce whenever he could, which was fresh and tasty. When her plate was empty and she was helping herself to seconds, Stella could no longer ignore the elephant in the room.

'What do you think about the job? First impressions, I mean…'

Rob nodded. 'It's tempting. To be honest, it's just what I've been looking for—a chance to take a step back on my own terms.'

'Maybe you shouldn't see it as a step back. It's a step forward into a place you've been before.'

'Yeah. Good thought. How do you feel about it? My working within the department.'

'You should make your own decision about this, Rob. What's best for you.'

He thought for a moment. 'Is there anything you need to tell me? Was this your idea, and Phil's just signed off on it?'

Time to come clean. It was a reasonable question, even if Stella wished he hadn't thought to ask it.

'I… This is all Phil's idea, although of course

I knew about it. Telling him I could deliver the documents by hand was just an excuse. Would you have turned up on my doorstep with the suggestion that we had sex?'

Rob chuckled. 'I probably would have made you read through a draft of my latest paper, and then bored you to tears with possible amendments before I worked up the nerve to mention it. Although, to be honest, I probably wouldn't have come at all. I know how much your work means to you, and how focused you are. You might not want to add a complication like me.'

The thought had occurred to her. But Stella had come because she wanted to. 'You're not a complication, Rob. You're far more...' she waved her hand, trying to find the right word '...far more complicated than that.'

He laughed. 'I'm glad you feel I'm more than just an ordinary complication. You're more complicated than a mere set of labels too.' He leaned back in his seat, clearly considering the matter, and Stella got to her feet, walking over to the coffee machine. They were going around in circles, and maybe they both needed to step back a bit and straighten things out.

'Here's the bottom line...' The second cup was filling before he spoke again, and when she turned Rob had the same look on his face that she'd seen when he was defining issues to do with Anna's case. If he was half as good at this as he was at surgery, then they were home free.

'I've learned to my cost that I can't have everything. You know that focusing on the area of your life that you most want is what works for you.'

'Yes. That's fair.'

'They're both good coping strategies. But neither of them is a universal truth, and they're not going to work if we use them as an excuse to keep us from the other things we want in life. We just have to respect each other's boundaries. I used to do your job, so I know exactly how to respect yours.'

'I want to be with you, Rob. Very much.'

He got to his feet, enveloping her in a hug. 'And I want to be with you. This is not too much to ask of life—people do manage to have jobs and relationships at the same time. It's not so easy when you have a job that's as all-consuming as yours, but we can make it easy. No recriminations over spending too much time at work...'

'You've had those too?' Stella twisted her mouth down.

'Yep. And maybe being involved in each other's professional lives, however much we keep that at arm's length from the personal, is going to be of some benefit. I'm proud of the work we did together on Anna's case, and Phil does mention that there's a potential for more of that kind of consultancy.'

Stella hadn't realised that Phil had included that as well—it must have been a last-minute revision after he'd spoken about the idea to Stella.

'I'm proud of it too. I'd like to think we could do it again some time.'

'What do you say, then? How *do* you feel about working with me?'

She'd thought that ducking the question, putting it to the back of her mind, was the right answer. Now Stella had a different response. She reached up, laying her fingers on the side of his face.

'I think it's a great opportunity for both of us. And that we can have a lot of fun compromising with each other.'

Who'd have thought that running away to a house in the country, and having sex for most of the weekend with the most gorgeous man she'd ever seen, would improve her work performance on Monday morning? But somehow the little niggles seemed less niggling than usual, and everything Stella touched seemed to go remarkably well. At lunchtime, Phil rapped on her door and blustered in, smiling.

'Just had a call from Rob. He says he's taking the job. He wants to add a few things to the scope of work, of course, but that's no particular surprise. He's signed the contracts and he'll be posting them back today.'

'That's great.' Phil didn't need to know that Rob

had signed the contracts yesterday, leaning them on her back. Then she'd felt the pen against her skin and she'd screamed in mock outrage, scattering the papers and snatching the pen from him. Pinning him down on the bed, she'd signed her own name between his shoulder blades, only to find when she looked in the mirror that, instead of his name, her skin bore a couple of entwined love hearts.

Phil was still rattling out the details, most of which Stella had already discussed with Rob. '... He'll be coming in on Thursday. I told him that it was unlikely we'd get the paperwork back by then, but he didn't seem too bothered about being paid on time...'

'No, I guess not. Phil, I asked him to mention...'

'About the two of you? Yes, he did.' Phil had a habit of delaying his reaction to anything until he'd heard people out. Clearly, he was waiting to see what else Stella had to say.

'Is that okay with you?'

'It's none of my business unless it affects your work, and you're both professional enough not to allow that to happen.' Phil smiled. 'Anything else?'

'No. Thanks, Phil, I really appreciate it.'

'It couldn't happen to two nicer people. I know that Rob's had his issues, but he's one of the best people I know. And if you ever want to chat—off the record—you know that I'm partial to a glass of orange juice at lunchtime.'

Stella nodded. Everyone knew that if they saw Phil drinking orange juice with another member of staff in the pub at lunchtime it was best to give them a wide berth, because Phil would be listening and dispensing a little wisdom. That was what made him such a good boss. The unit was personally loyal to him as well as professionally loyal, and Stella had always tried to follow his example with her own team.

'I'll bear that in mind. Rob's one of the best people I know too. As well as being a very gifted surgeon.'

'No arguments there. It's good to have him back here on a more regular basis.' Phil breezed out of the room, clearly happy that he'd achieved whatever he'd set out to do.

'Miss me?' Rob appeared in her office at eight-thirty on Thursday morning.

'No.' Stella laughed at his expression of dismay. 'How can I miss you when I'm still tingling?'

'Good point. I had a set of small and completely painless bruises to comfort me in your absence.'

'You did? I wasn't aware of having bruised you.'

'As I said, they were small and painless.' He rubbed his arm and Stella vaguely remembered clinging on to it for dear life at one point. 'I would have barely noticed them if they hadn't been something I felt sentimentally attached to.'

'Right. Think you're over them now, or do I need to take a look?'

'You were the one that brought tingling up. Want me to take a look at that?'

Touché. 'We'll neither of us take a look at anything. I shouldn't have even mentioned it since we're at work.'

Rob grinned, sitting down in the seat opposite her desk. 'I'm not at work yet. I don't start until nine in the morning.'

'Sadly, I am. What can I do for you, Mr Franklin?' Stella shot him her most professional smile, which didn't seem to faze him in the slightest.

'Rob, please. I think first names are okay between colleagues. I hear that Anna's coming in this morning.'

'I have an appointment with her at eleven. I've mentioned it to Phil, as he was hoping to spend some time with you before lunch, and I reckoned you'd want to check up on Anna as well.'

'Thanks. Would you mind if Ottilie sits in on that? She wrote a cracking report on the surgery, and she's hoping it'll count towards her marks for this part of her course.'

'I've already asked her to get me the results of Anna's scans and X-rays, and told her that if Anna's okay with her staying it's fine with me. Ottilie's still a bit rough around the edges, but she's turning out to be really helpful to everyone in Theatre, and I thought she might like to follow through with Anna.'

'Perfect. I'll just go home now, shall I? Since you appear to have organised everything.'

'Don't you dare. I think Phil's got something up his sleeve that he needs some help with. We're a surgeon down this week.'

Rob grinned broadly. He was never happier than when he was on the move, and busy suited him. 'I'll get out of your hair, then. See you later.'

Ottilie knocked on her door at a quarter to eleven sharp, proffering a tablet with all of the information that Stella needed. She flipped through the X-rays, thinking aloud for Ottilie's benefit. 'The real test is when we see her face, nothing replaces that. But from here I can see that the implants are beginning to knit well and I'm hopeful. We need to be very honest about our prognosis, but at the same time we can obviously give Anna the encouragement she needs. She's been through a lot to get this far.'

Ottilie nodded.

'I want you to have these X-rays ready for me or Mr Franklin to refer to during the consultation, but don't show them to Anna or any members of the family unless I tell you to. Anna's usually interested to see scans and X-rays, but we have to be sensitive to her needs on this particular day. I want you to be responsible for making sure that the information's there when we need it, but that the screen's off when we don't.'

'Thank you. I'll do that, Ms Parry-Jones.'

'Good. You haven't seen Mr Franklin around anywhere, have you?'

'I think he's in with Mr Chamberlain.' Ottilie had clearly made sure that she had an answer for everything. 'Would you like me to knock?'

'Yes, get him along to Procedure Room Three when you find him, will you? I'm going to see how Anna's doing…'

The nurse had already administered an analgesic, removed the outer bandages and moistened the inner pad to make sure that it could be removed without traumatising the area of the grafts. It was an uncomfortable process, but Jess was there, holding Anna's hand and talking to her.

'Hey there, Jess. How are you feeling today, Anna?'

'A bit scared. Today's the day, isn't it.' Anna's speech was slurred by emotion as well as the fact that her jaw was still very tender.

It was an important day. Not the only day… 'This is a long process, Anna. We'll be able to see a little more today, because the swelling's gone down now, but you've still got quite a bit of healing to do.'

'It's going to be difficult to see at first. But we can take the docs' word for it and use our imaginations,' Jess chimed in. 'I know you're scared, though. I am too.'

'We're going to wait until the dressing's moist enough and… Ah, here's Mr Franklin.' The door had opened and Rob appeared, closely followed by Ottilie, who sat down on a chair in the corner.

Anna waved her hand, unable to move her head to see Rob properly, but Jess got to her feet and made straight for Ottilie. The two young women exchanged a few words and Ottilie seemed to be trying to persuade Jess to go back to sit with Anna, clutching the tablet against her chest so that Jess would have no chance of seeing it.

Rob turned. 'Is there a problem?'

'No…' Ottilie waved Jess away again.

'There's no problem at all.' Jess could always be relied upon to make her feelings known. 'Ottilie found us and brought us sandwiches and coffee when Anna was in the operating theatre. Then some soup later on, and she stayed and chatted with Anna's dad about his crossword—he couldn't concentrate on it but he wouldn't put it down and I'm no good with cryptic clues. I never got the chance to thank her—'

'I didn't say anything. About how the operation was going.' Ottilie interrupted Jess, reddening furiously and clearly worried that Rob might think she'd done something wrong. There were lots of reasons why information about patients was carefully controlled, and Stella hoped that Ottilie hadn't given in to the temptation to give Anna's family an incomplete and possibly incorrect assessment of how Anna's surgery was progressing.

Jess could see that something was up. 'Was it wrong of me to ask how Anna was doing? I'm sorry, but the waiting was really getting to me…'

Rob stepped in. 'Please don't stop asking questions, Jess. I'd be heartbroken.' Anna's shoulders were shaking with laughter now, and she gave Rob's retort a thumbs-up.

'Well, Ottilie couldn't give me an answer anyway. She said that she knew it was hard but we had to wait, because the only people who could tell us what we needed to know were the surgeons who were operating. But that's beside the point. What I *really* wanted to tell Ottilie was that I was so busy worrying about Anna that I never gave her the money for the food she brought us.'

Rob nodded, clearly happy with the situation. 'That was a very kind gesture, Ottilie, thank you.'

'I went to the hospital kitchen and they gave me some leftovers; it didn't cost me anything.' Ottilie smiled at Jess. 'I didn't think you'd remember me.'

Rob raised his eyebrows, obviously thinking the same as Stella. Ottilie still had a lot to learn. She'd gone out of her way to try and comfort Jess and Anna's parents on one of the worst days of their lives. Of course Jess remembered her kindness.

But they couldn't keep Anna waiting any longer. 'There'll be plenty of time to talk later on. Are you ready to start now, Anna?' Stella received a thumbs-up in reply, and turned towards the basin to wash her hands.

Peeling the dressings back from Anna's face and neck had to be done carefully, and then there was the matter of how to concentrate on what she saw, without creating an awkward silence that would leave Anna wondering what was happening. Rob made that a lot easier, stationing himself where Anna could see him and murmuring words of encouragement, while Stella got on with inspecting the healing skin grafts and checking Anna's jaw was aligned properly.

Now it was just a matter of resisting the temptation to punch the air and hug Anna, and give her a more professional assessment.

'I'm really pleased with your progress, Anna. You're healing well and the shape of your jaw is much better now.'

Anna gave an emphatic thumbs-up, slurring out a few words. 'I want to see.'

'Okay. That's fine. Now, remember that the skin's looking very discoloured still, that's to be expected, and it's an indication that there's a good blood supply to the grafts. Your jaw is still a little swollen, so don't expect any miracles just yet.'

Anna nodded. 'Let me see.'

Rob carefully raised the head of the couch, bringing Anna up into a sitting position. Stella signalled to Ottilie to fetch the mirror from the cupboard and hold it up for Anna. She grinned, knowing that this was a special privilege.

There was silence for a moment, everyone waiting as Anna stared at her reflection. Stella gave her a little time to take everything in, and then began to carefully explain.

'You see here, the shape of your jaw on the left side matches the right. As I said, the skin grafts are discoloured—'

Anna waved her away. She understood. Her eyes filled with tears, and Stella quickly wiped her left eye so that they shouldn't fall onto her cheek.

'I look like me.'

Battered, bruised and swollen, and with a lot of healing ahead of her. But Anna was right. Something about the shape of her face did suggest the young woman that Stella had seen in the photographs from before the accident, which Jess and her parents had provided.

'Beautiful. You look beautiful, sweetheart.' Tears were streaming down Jess's face and Rob reached for a box of tissues.

Stella couldn't help shooting a secret grin in his direction. This was the moment. The one that made the long hours of preparation and the careful, painstaking work all worth it. And Rob saw that too, he understood. He knew that if she worked at weekends, or late into the evening, this was the result she was reaching for. All of the broken relationships, the partners who hadn't understood why she had to focus so fiercely on her work… They didn't matter any more because Rob was here, sharing this moment with her.

Stella had quickly taken some photographs for the file, and Anna had passed her phone over to Ottilie, so that she could take some of her and Jess together. Then Stella had re-dressed Anna's face for the last time. The next time she came to see her, Stella expected that the grafts would be healed enough not to need any protection. Jess had said her thankyous once again, and she'd left Rob and Ottilie to take Anna and Jess through to the unit's patient lounge, where Anna would be able to sit for a while until she was ready to go home.

She didn't see him again until the evening. Rob had texted her, saying he'd meet her at a nearby café, and she found him sitting outside, under a flapping sunshade in the large paved area which overlooked the banks of the river. The last of the rush-hour commuters were snaking their way along the pavement below, their heads turned down, and Rob was watching the boats. Stella usually went straight home after work, but this seemed a better way to spend her time than crushed up against a gazillion people in an underground train.

'How was your afternoon?' She sat down and Rob signalled to the waitress, catching her attention to order another cup of coffee for himself, and tea for Stella.

'Good.' He grinned. 'Terrifying.'

'How so?'

'You reckon you have the knack of thinking aloud when you have a student in tow?' She nodded. 'Yeah, so did I. It's a bit different when you have thirty of them, all staring at you, and no patient to concentrate on. It's like being in a tank of piranhas.'

Stella laughed. 'Don't exaggerate. They're not going to eat you.'

'Maybe not. But I had to keep my wits about me; they're quite capable of sucking me dry for information. You remember what it was like when you were a student? They used to call it a keenness to learn.'

'And did they?'

'You'd have been proud of the way I fought back. Yeah, they learned. I took in a bag of bananas…'

Stella chuckled. She remembered carefully stitching the skin of a banana when she'd been a student. 'Don't they have any artificial skin pads in the stock cupboard?'

'Yep. But I'll let them have them when they get it perfect on a banana. They're on student grants, so they're much cheaper to practice at home with, and you can eat the banana afterwards so…' He waved his hand. 'You know. Magnesium, Potassium, Vitamin B6…'

'So they'll be well nourished and clamouring to try out their perfect stitching by the time they're allowed into Theatre. Thanks a lot, Rob.'

'I've added that to my lesson plans. I'll bark out orders and they have to read my mind, run around and keep out of each other's way. It's going to be a non-compulsory session.'

'Is anyone going to turn up?' Non-compulsory sessions were traditionally a bit more interesting than learning how not to bump into people, even if that was a very necessary skill.

'We'll see. I had a video-conferencing session with Phil and the head of the teaching faculty during the week. Phil's exact words were *"Good luck with it"*.'

'I can't believe you don't know what he means by that.' The waitress had arrived with their drinks, and Stella took a sip of her tea. Sitting down with a cup of tea after work always helped her to switch off for whatever remained of the evening, and doing it here, with Rob, instead of at home on her own, was far more effective.

'We'll see. I'm taking the unspoken *It's never going to work* part as a challenge.' Rob was still smiling, but there was a flash of grey-blue steel in his eyes.

'Well…good luck with it, then.' Stella grinned at him, swallowing down the temptation to ask why Rob hadn't found the time to video-conference with *her*. That was new. Her partners' absences from a relationship had generally been something of a relief, because they'd diverted attention from her own.

'So...lecturing. What else?'

'I filled in with a couple of short procedures in Theatre since we're understaffed, attended a planning meeting and did Phil's ward rounds for him while he was in Theatre.'

'So you took it easy since it's your first day.' It was no particular surprise that Rob had hit the ground running. He probably reckoned it was just a brisk jogging pace.

'Are we going to talk about ears?' He was on to the next thing now.

'Anna's ear, you mean? No, not right now. Maybe never. At the moment she's content with her ear the way it is. She's already had enough surgery to last most people a lifetime, and there may well be a few more corrective procedures ahead of her.' This was new too. Usually, Stella was quite ruthless about separating her work from her leisure time, but she could trust that Rob's reaction wouldn't be incomprehension or mild horror at the details.

'Your restraint is commendable. It's a pretty straightforward earlobe repair.'

'And it's *her* earlobe. I'm not going to encourage her either way.'

'You're right, of course. It's exactly what I'd do, but I wouldn't be able to help a bit of private frustration over not getting things as perfect as I could for her.' He frowned suddenly, taking a sip of his coffee. 'I might have caught myself out there. I was reckoning that I wouldn't fall into that trap again this time.'

'Would you have even seen it before?' Stella was seeing her own life a little more clearly since she'd met Rob.

'Nah, probably not. There's a lot of mental energy involved in making every aspect of your life perfect. Not a lot of time for anything else.' He thought for a moment. 'Jess sees Anna as perfect already.'

'No, she doesn't. Jess doesn't need perfect because she sees Anna as beautiful. That's different.' Stella had spent more time with Anna and Jess and got to know them better than Rob did.

'Yeah. That's an interesting point.' He was tracing his finger around the handle of his cup, and there was obviously something more bothering him.

'What?'

'It's just… Are you okay? Really okay, I mean. We're turning each other's lives upside down… I'm chipping away at your focus…'

That wasn't arrogance on Rob's part; they both knew the impact they'd had on each other. Keeping everything else secondary to her job had always worked for Stella, and Rob *was* challenging that at the moment. His guilt over wanting to have everything, and then finding that was the most destructive thing possible, made him unsure too.

'I'm okay. It's new territory for me, but you're a surgeon. You understand the focus.'

He nodded, clearly reassured. 'What do you say we skip the nice meal at a little restaurant I happen to know? The champagne and strawberries and a surprise red rose in the taxi home...'

'Champagne and strawberries would have been lovely, and the rose is a really nice touch. But it is a weeknight. What do you have in mind?'

He moved his hand across the table, his fingers meeting hers. The slight pressure of his thumb was a lot more intoxicating than mere champagne. 'Get the tube back to your flat. Feel our skin touch.'

'That sounds beautiful, Rob.'

The word *beautiful* wasn't lost on him. He laughed, signalling to the waitress for the bill.

# CHAPTER TWELVE

THERE HAD BEEN a beginning, but he and Stella had no defined aims, no particular point where they needed to end up. It was a new experience for Rob, but he was thriving on it.

He'd decided that a date—a proper date where they dressed up a bit and went somewhere—was his next step. He'd booked some theatre tickets, a long-running West End thriller, and bought a suit with him when he came down to London the following week. A pre-theatre meal was going to be a rush, as Stella never got away from work on time on a Friday evening, but he reckoned that a post-theatre meal would work, and that since he wasn't on call on Saturday they'd be able to sleep in as long as they wanted.

'You scrub up *very* well, Rob.' He'd showered and changed at work, so that he could arrive at her place in a taxi to pick her up. She met him on the front doorstep of her block of flats, promptly taking his breath away.

The classic little black dress took on a whole new meaning when Stella wore it, because her red hair and green eyes gave all the intensity of colour and the subtlety of shade that was needed.

She took his arm and he led her down the steps outside the building.

'You look absolutely stunning. I'm beginning to wish that I'd been there to watch you dress.' He murmured the words into her ear before they got into the taxi.

'Thank you.'

Rob waited for the expected comment about him being there to watch her undress but it never came. Stella seemed a little subdued, but maybe she was just tired. Perhaps Rob should have waited for tickets on Saturday evening instead, but this was the play they both wanted to see, and Friday tickets had been the only ones that were available. She checked her phone in the theatre foyer, typing a text and then nodding silently when the reply pinged back.

The play was great. Witty and suspenseful, with beautiful costumes and sets. The interval came round too soon, leaving the audience to chatter about the cliff-hanger they'd been faced with as they left their seats. Stella's hand disappeared into her handbag as they walked towards the crowded bar, and she seemed to be trying to surreptitiously switch her phone on.

'Stop right there.' He caught her arm, guiding her to a less busy spot, and Stella snatched her hand from her bag guiltily. 'What's up?'

'Nothing… Nothing at all. Theo Vasilis is looking after a patient of mine and he said he'd text me if there was any news.' She pulled her phone out of her bag, switching it on and showing it to him. 'Look. No news. Let's see if we can elbow our way across to the bar, shall we?'

'You want to call him?'

Yeah. She did. Rob could tell because he'd been right there in her shoes, many times.

'No, it's fine. Theo will be looking after her. I never have any worries about patients of mine who are in his care. We both spoke with her husband after the operation and I handed over all the notes…'

'Okay. Why are you so keen to follow up on this patient?' He glanced over at the bar. 'We're not going to get served at the moment, so you may as well indulge my curiosity.'

'Young woman with a cyst on her neck, Aarya. She'd had it for a little while and was going to get it removed, but then she found out she was pregnant and decided to wait until after she'd had the baby. She came back in for the surgery today— the cyst was quite large and it needed a general anaesthetic.'

'And…'

'The anaesthetist had a little trouble stabilising her, just as I was about to close. I stopped and made sure that she was all right, then we finished up. She came round from the anaesthetic with no problems at all.'

No surgery went entirely smoothly, because they

were dealing with people and a delicate balance of many different factors. Stella had done everything correctly and according to the book. Rob knew all of that, but he also knew that had he been in Stella's place, he would have wanted to stick around for a while as well.

He took her arm, propelling her through the foyer and out of the theatre. Then a golden taxi drew up alongside them, its 'For Hire' sign alight. Rob hesitated, wondering whether he was witnessing a miracle, and then realised that it was one of the taxis that had been resprayed to celebrate the Queen's Golden Jubilee, and that finding an empty taxi so quickly on a Friday evening was just exceptionally good luck. He signalled to the driver and opened the door, ushering Stella firmly inside.

'The Thames Hospital, please,' he said firmly, and the driver pulled away from the pavement.

'Rob, there's no need. We can turn round now and catch the second half of the play.' She was protesting loudly and the taxi driver slowed, clearly wondering whether he was about to be asked to perform a U-turn.

'It's okay.' Rob caught the driver's attention. 'If she kills me, just take her to the nearest police station.'

Stella laughed suddenly and the taxi driver chuckled. 'Right you are, mate.' The taxi sped up again, making for the hospital.

'Don't give me that look.' Stella had stopped

protesting out loud now. 'I can't count the number of evenings that I've raced home in the nick of time, and spent a whole evening somewhere worrying about a patient. Trying to put on a show of enjoying myself, when I'd really rather be at the hospital. Kate would be shooting me reproachful looks, and I'd be feeling guilty about not being able to be in two places at once. I don't want to be on either side of that again, not with you.'

Stella pressed her lips together. 'I know that she'll be all right.'

'Of course she's all right. But we're all human—something happens and a patient suddenly pushes all of your buttons and you want to stick around. The same way we stuck around for Anna when there wasn't really anything more we could do for her.'

She nodded. 'I suppose so. Aarya brought her new baby with her when she came in for the pre-op examination, and she was just gorgeous. And her husband was clearly worried about her when we went to find him afterwards. I just wanted to make everything go well for them all, I suppose. I'm so sorry, Rob.'

'You've already made everything go well. And you don't need to apologise to me. I'm a doctor, remember? I said that I didn't want to put myself in between you and your work, and this was exactly what I meant. That we're both free to enjoy our time together because we're not being torn in two all the time.'

Stella leaned over and kissed him on the cheek, the caress of her fingers making him shiver. Maybe Rob had overreacted a bit, but he'd made Stella smile again.

And maybe he hadn't been quite as unreliable as Kate had liked to make out. She'd known what she was getting when she'd married him, and the things that Rob had been working so hard for were things she'd wanted too. He'd never reproached her for anything, and he wouldn't now, even in the privacy of his own mind—but there *had* been a breakdown in communication between them.

Stella insisted on paying for the taxi, giving the driver a broad grin, and laughing when he joked about his relief that there had been no deaths in the back of his taxi. They walked into the hospital side by side, ignoring whatever whispers and second glances followed them, and made their way up to Stella's office.

She took off her watch and bracelet and put on her doctor's white coat, more to disguise the dress than anything else. Rob took off his jacket and tie and rolled up his sleeves. They made their way down to the post-operative suite and Stella beckoned to a young doctor, who came hurrying over.

'We were just passing.' That probably didn't fool anyone, but it saved face. 'How's Aarya been?'

'Fine. I had a nurse sitting with her but she wasn't

184 COUNTRY FLING WITH THE CITY SURGEON

needed. We let her husband in for a few minutes and he's gone home now. I think she's still awake if you want to check in on her.'

'Thanks, Theo. I really appreciate it.'

Theo chuckled, nodding. In Rob's experience, most surgeons just breezed into post-operative wards without bothering to check in with anyone, and Stella's courtesy had clearly earned Theo's respect.

It took a moment for his eyes to adjust to the subdued lighting in the cubicle, but when they did he could see that Aarya was awake. Stella approached her bedside, a smile on her face.

'How are you doing? Your neck's a bit stiff, I imagine.' There was a large dressing on the side of Aarya's neck.

'I'm fine. They gave me some tablets and it doesn't hurt.'

'That's good.' Stella sat down by the bed. 'Everything else okay?'

'Yes, I saw Dipak. I told him to go home now.' Aarya turned the corners of her mouth down.

'I bet you're missing your baby.'

'It's the first time I've been away from her. Do you think Dipak will be able to bring her into the ward tomorrow?'

'I'll ask for you. You may have to go out into the visitors room to see her, but the staff here will organise everything. And you'll be going home to her soon. The best thing you can do now is get some sleep and feel better in the morning…'

Rob slipped out of the room, taking the patient notes with him, so that he could flip through them and report back to Stella. She appeared through the curtains ten minutes later, shooting him a reproachful look as she took the notes out of his hand and went back to replace them at the end of the bed.

'Everything okay?'

'Yes, she's sleeping now. Are her notes okay?' Stella just couldn't resist asking.

'Absolutely fine. Nothing to worry about.'

Stella signalled a goodbye to Theo on the way out, and they walked back up to her office. Taking off her white coat, she picked up her handbag from the desk while Rob rolled down his sleeves and put on his tie. They were ready for date night part two.

'Thank you, Rob.' Stella put her arms around his neck, kissing him. 'I really appreciate this. And I'm sorry we missed out on finding out who did it…'

'It's my pleasure. We'll go again another time and catch the end of the play, and as for tonight— we're in time for our dinner reservation.'

She kissed him again. This was turning into a perfect date because they'd done everything they both needed to, and done it together. Suddenly,

Stella stepped back from him. 'I smell of soap, don't I?'

'Yes, you do.' He pulled her back towards him, kissing her for one last time before he pulled on his jacket. 'Don't you know by now that I *love* the smell of soap...'

# CHAPTER THIRTEEN

THERE HAD BEEN nine perfect weekends, spent at Rob's house in Sussex. Sunny days, hot sultry nights and Rob to share them with. Stella sometimes needed to bring some work with her, but they would sit down together in the conservatory office and he'd work on his teaching plans or research notes, while she logged in to the secure hospital network and reviewed patient files and answered emails. It was companionable and easy, Sophie sleeping in her basket under the cool greenery and only waking up if a butterfly got too close to her nose.

It was a lot easier to finish work when Rob was around as well. There was none of that clinging worry that usually came when she closed her laptop on a Saturday afternoon, because there were farm shops to visit and then the local supermarket. Saturday evenings were for cooking and eating, often in the garden as the sun went down. On Sundays they'd go exploring. Rob had visited surprisingly few places of interest in the area, and so they could discover them together.

And shot through all of it was the excitement of his kiss. The brush of his fingers on her bare arm, the feeling of lazy delight when she woke in the morning, knowing that they wouldn't be getting up until Rob's slow caress had put the finishing touches to a night where desire dictated everything. Curling up with him afterwards, until the sun made it impossible for them to stay in bed any longer.

This weekend, though, there was no work before they could relax and play. Rob was already loading up his car when she arrived, and Stella took the sparkly silver envelope from the glove compartment.

She kissed him, and then batted away his questions about what she'd been up to this week, and gave him the envelope. Rob opened it, reading the card inside, and a broad grin spread across his face.

'That's really nice.'

'Isn't it? I got a card too, only my envelope's pink.'

Ottilie had done well in her end of term assessments and had sent them gorgeous thank you notes. They'd expected that, because Rob had written a glowing report on her practical work, but her case studies and other academic work had attracted top marks as well.

Rob nodded with satisfaction. 'She deserves it.'

'Yes, I told her that. And I said that we were looking forward to working with her again.'

'That's great. I'm going to put this on the mantelpiece right now…'

Rob disappeared into the house, while Stella regarded the collection of seemingly unrelated items in the boot of his car. He was still smiling when he re-joined her.

'Have you got room for three more boxes?'

'Three? Where did you get three boxes of books from?'

'I put an empty box on the table in the hallway of my block of flats, with a note saying that any unwanted books would be appreciated, and that they were being sold in aid of an adult literacy scheme. The first box filled in under a day and I had to go down to the corner shop and ask if they had another.'

'Nice one.' Rob walked with her to her car, and she opened the boot. He pulled the packing tape off one of the boxes and started to poke around amongst the contents. 'This is really good… I haven't read this one.'

'Put it back.' Stella tapped the back of his hand with her fingers. 'If you want it, you'll have to pay for it like everyone else.'

Rob dropped the book back into the box, propping it on top of one of the other boxes and ferrying them to his own car. Stella brought the last box, which had to go on the back seat because there was no room for it in the boot.

'Do you really need those pieces of wood for a village fete?'

'Might do. There weren't enough tables to go round and I built a stall for Emma, along with a board at the back for her to pin up her notices about the literacy scheme. She might want a few alterations. I said I'd pick her up on the way, she's got a few more boxes of books as well.'

'Okay, I'll go in the back with the boxes, and Emma can go in the front seat.' Stella looked around. 'Where's Sophie?'

'Ah… I'm going to need her basket as well. She'll want a snooze. Maybe I should go and get the roof rack.'

They finally managed to get everything into the car and set off for the village, stopping along the way to pick up Emma. When they arrived at the large grassy area behind the church it was bustling with activity. Emma's stall turned out to be a stoutly built affair, with a brightly painted sign and plenty of room for the leaflets and posters she'd brought along with her.

'I didn't know that you were involved with an adult literacy scheme, Emma.' Emma had sorted the books according to what she thought they would all fetch, and Stella was busy writing the prices inside the front covers.

'Oh, yes. I have been for years. I used to be a teacher, you know. Still am, I suppose. You never quite stop doing something you love.'

'I suppose that's okay if you're a teacher. I can't see myself having a stall at a village fete doing scar reduction.'

Emma chuckled. 'That would be something new. Rob seems to be finding a use for his talents.'

Stella looked across to where Rob was safely out of earshot, patching up one of the old tables with some of the wooden lathes he'd brought. That wasn't quite the same thing, but it seemed to involve the concentration and care that surgery took, even if the tools weren't the same.

'He was in a very bad state when he first came here,' Emma mused, almost to herself. 'It was months before any of us even saw him.'

Stella nodded. 'Yes, I know.' Emma was clearly fond of Rob and she was a shrewd judge of human nature. This wasn't idle gossip, and it must have been obvious that Rob wasn't well when he'd first arrived here.

'I'm glad he's found you. It's about time he started to go back out in the world again.' Emma had opened Rob's box of books and was sorting them into piles for Stella to price up. 'What's this one? *Crypto...*'

Stella glanced up at the book. 'Cryptotia. It's where the ear doesn't develop properly. I'm not sure that anyone's going to be much interested in that, he might have put it in there by mistake.'

'We'll put that to one side then, you never know when it might come in handy. How much should we sell this one for? It's already been read at least twice, because Rob lent it to me.'

'A pound. You're obviously both careful with

your books because it looks almost new. And look at the price on the back. I bet someone would give a pound for it.'

'I was thinking twenty-five pence.' Emma thought for a moment. 'But you're right, someone will give a pound and it's all for a good cause. Perhaps you should price all of the twenty-five pence ones as fifty pence instead. If I see someone who I know can't afford much, I can always give them a discount, can't I?'

Emma knew practically everyone in the village, and had probably taught many of them. And she'd welcomed Stella here, always stopping to say hello and talk for a while when they bumped into each other in the shop or the main street, which happened quite often because Emma went shopping every day, around the same time that Rob usually walked down to get his paper.

'How *was* Rob when he first came here?' It felt wrong somehow to ask, but Emma was as protective of Rob as she felt. And she couldn't help herself.

Emma laid the books she was sorting down in her lap. 'He was in an awful state. So thin, and when I found him shovelling snow in the high street he jumped nearly a mile when I tapped him on the shoulder. Burned out, I'd say. He did what he was told but he wouldn't take the initiative with anything.'

Stella had known all this, but Emma's description brought it all home far more clearly.

'He told me you set him to work, getting people's shopping.'

'Well, yes, I did. We had plenty of volunteers, we always do, but I thought it might do him a bit of good. Something that he could get his teeth into and succeed with. In my experience, failure can eat into a person and it's not too difficult in those circumstances to blame yourself for everything.'

'You never said you were a detective.' Stella wondered what Emma thought of her, but decided she probably wouldn't say.

Emma laughed. 'All schoolteachers need to be detectives. You have thirty faces in front of you, and not very long to decide what makes each one of them tick. Rob Franklin wasn't all that hard to work out.'

Maybe not, if you were as perceptive as Emma. The inside of an operating theatre *did* teach you a bit about human nature, but not in quite the same way.

'You're very kind, Emma.'

Emma waved the comment away, although Stella could see that it pleased her. 'It's nice to see two people making a fresh start.'

Two people? Stella supposed that she was making a fresh start of sorts, but hers didn't involve the long road that Rob had travelled. She must have shown her surprise, because Emma shot her a knowing look.

'Come here. You've left the price tag on your dress, right at the back of your neck. It's such a pretty dress and it quite spoils it. I'll cut it out for you...'

Rob had finished shoring up a few tables, and was now carrying the sunshades out of the storeroom at the back of the church hall. Deciding that Emma could probably do with one of them, he walked over to where she and Stella were arranging books on the stall. There was clearly a bit of discussion going on, and he imagined that neither of them was about to give way on exactly how they should classify them.

'Shall I fix your sunshade, Emma?'

'Thank you, Rob. The sun is getting a little hot. I could do with a cool drink.'

'I'll go and fetch you one when I've finished.' Rob hauled the heavy base into place, and started to fix the sunshade onto the curved support.

'I've got one of your books here, Rob. I'm not sure that we'll have much of a call for books on cryptotia this afternoon.' Emma enunciated the medical term carefully.

He glanced at Stella, and she avoided his gaze. Clearly, she wasn't going to take any part in this conversation.

'No, probably not. I don't know how that got in

there; it was in my recycling pile.' Emma raised her eyebrows. 'It's a little out of date. Things change pretty quickly.'

'If it's out of date, Rob, it's not going to be much use to anyone,' Emma rebuked him gently and waved the book at him. Stella came to his rescue, grabbing the book while he finished adjusting the sunshade.

'How's that?'

'Very nice. Thank you. I'm going to need all of my wits about me this afternoon, because Stella and I have decided that we're going to drive a hard bargain with our customers. We've priced everything at more than fifty pence.'

So Stella was on Emma's team now, was she? That was pretty much par for the course and Stella didn't seem to mind. Rob didn't either; it was nice to see her getting to know people here.

'Good call. Most people can afford fifty pence.'

'Emma's going to give me a nudge if she sees anyone who can't. We'll give them a discount. But we want to make as much money as we can, because it's such a good cause and the scheme needs to buy more teaching materials.' Stella grinned at him.

So, presumably, if he wanted to see Stella at all today he was going to have to help out on the book-stall. Emma had probably already thought of that.

'What would you like to drink? Some orange-ade, or tea?'

'Actually, I think I'll go inside, Rob. We have a couple of hours before things start in earnest, and I wouldn't mind a quiet cup of tea and a nap in the church lounge before I leap into the fray.'

He watched as Emma walked across the grass, towards the church.

'Emma's really kind, isn't she?' Stella murmured.

'Yeah. Smarter than most as well…' Rob turned, suddenly aware of a commotion coming from the refreshment tent. One of the women who'd been cutting cakes and sandwiches appeared, making a beeline for him, and he walked towards her.

'Anything the matter, Cathy?'

'Yes, Janice has cut herself. You couldn't come and have a look at it, could you? It probably needs a bandage or something.'

'No problem, my medical bag's in my car.' Rob always kept it with him when he was on call.

'I'll fetch it for you.' Stella nudged him and he gave her the car keys.

Janice had been one of his first patients when he'd started work as a GP here, a young woman expecting her first child. Her little boy was sitting on one of the women's laps at the far end of the refreshment tent, and Rob realised he knew the names of all of the children in the makeshift crèche. It occurred to him to wonder for a moment whether the difference between his two jobs—his two lifestyles—was as apparent to Stella as it was to him right now.

He sat down opposite Janice, giving her a smile. She had a pad of kitchen towel wound tightly around her thumb, and from the look of her apron the wound had been bleeding freely.

'Hi, Janice. How are you doing?'

'If I let go, it just starts to bleed again.'

'Okay, just keep hold of it for a moment. Do you feel dizzy or sick?'

Janice shook her head. 'No, it was a bit of a shock, but I feel okay.'

Stella must have hurried to catch him up, because he heard her voice behind him and the buzz of the zip on his medical bag. He turned and she held out a wipe for him to disinfect his hands and then a pair of surgical gloves. Perfect, seamless synchronicity, as if one world had intruded on another for a moment and the sounds and smells of the operating theatre were about to overwhelm the sound of children playing and the scent of newly baked cake on a warm Saturday afternoon. Rob peeled back the kitchen towel, hastily reapplying pressure when blood started to drip from the wound.

'Bit more pressure, I think…'

He checked the wound again quickly to make sure that there was nothing in it, and Stella passed him a wad of gauze. He applied more pressure, raising Janice's hand above her head.

'You're pretty well kitted out,' Stella murmured as they waited.

'Yeah, you'd be surprised how many cuts I see. It saves everyone's time to do this myself, rather than send someone down to the small injuries clinic if they need a couple of stitches.'

After ten minutes, the bleeding still hadn't stopped. Cathy unlocked the church kitchen and Stella wiped the table down with disinfectant, before opening the wound care pack and laying the dressings out on a sterile sheet, while Rob cleaned the wound and checked again whether there was anything in it. The two stitches and applying a sterile dressing took less time than it did for him to write down the wound care instructions for Janice.

'Give the surgery a call on Monday and make an appointment with me for the following Monday to take out the stiches. In the meantime, keep the wound covered with the dressings I've given you and if there are any of the indications of infection that I've listed out, give me a call straight away.'

'Thank you. Can I go back and help with the refreshments?'

'I'd give that a rest for today. You've done your share, go and enjoy the fete.'

They cleared up the mess, dropping it all into a plastic bag. Stella's shoulders were shaking with laughter. 'Overkill or what, eh? Two surgeons for a couple of stitches.'

Rob shrugged. 'No such thing as having too many surgeons. Anyway, I'm a GP here.'

She looked up at him. 'You're still a surgeon,

Rob. You've proved that beyond any shadow of a doubt.'

It seemed important to her that he should classify himself that way. Rob could understand that; she'd worked hard for the title and she had a right to be proud of it.

'I…don't really feel as if I am.'

'I think that Anna might beg to differ. I certainly would. And so would your students.'

'It's different. I know a lot about surgery, and I still have the skills. I'm not sure that I could do it every day, like you do.'

She seemed deflated suddenly, sitting down with a bump on one of the kitchen chairs. 'What is this?'

Rob sat down next to her. 'There's a lot I can do. I can pass on my knowledge, I can help plan and execute surgeries. That's a lot more than I felt I could do three months ago, and I have you to thank—'

'No. You have *yourself* to thank,' Stella interrupted him.

'Whatever. I told you when we first started that I wasn't sure I had it in me any more to be able to work full-time as a surgeon, and I'm still not sure.'

He could practically see the cogs whirring in her brain. He wanted to reach out and touch her face, do something to change the subject to a lighter topic, but experience told him that once Stella took hold of something, she didn't let go that easily.

'You think that you let people down? Still?'

'I *did* let people down. I allowed myself to get to a place where I just couldn't function. I couldn't pull myself together...'

She brought her hand down onto the table with such a bang that they both jumped. 'Don't you dare! You were diagnosed as suffering from stress and clinical depression, and no one can be expected to just pull themselves together in those circumstances. If you ever said that to one of your patients, you'd be in real trouble. So don't say it to yourself.'

'Hey. Are you giving me a hard time?'

'Yes, I am. Because you give me a hard time when you think I'm doing something wrong. I wish you could see how far you've come in the last few months, and know that you can go a lot further.'

'I see it. And I hear what you're saying, Stella. Maybe you should just keep wearing me down.' Like cool water flowing across obstinate rock. If Stella stayed with him, then maybe one day he'd start to believe that he could take the risk of moving forward without letting her down.

'Is that a challenge?' She shot him a mischievous look.

'Yeah. Please do take it as one.' He leaned forward, planting a kiss onto her lips. That made him feel a lot better, because Stella's lips could chase away all of his fears and insecurities.

'I'm not going to forget all about this just because you're kissing me...'

'No?' He kissed her again. 'You're sure about that?' He knew one way to make them both forget about everything. But they had a fete to attend before they'd be alone.

She gave a mock sigh. 'All right. We're just going to have to agree to differ for the time being then.'

'And in the meantime I bet I can sell more books than you...'

'Really?' She drew back from him, folding her arms. 'You think so?'

'I've read a few of them. When did you last have the time to sit down and read a book, cover to cover? Medical books don't count.'

'So I'll just read the blurb on the back and say it sounds interesting. How does Emma do it?'

'We're not even in Emma's league. Last year people were just picking up a couple of books, giving her a note and telling her to keep the change. Everyone knows it's for a good cause. You, on the other hand... I reckon I can beat you.'

'I'll be interested in watching you try.' She got to her feet, plumping herself back down on his knee and kissing him. 'I'll be pulling out all the stops, Rob.'

Fair enough. That was all Rob needed. The future could look after itself, as long as she was here for him today.

# CHAPTER FOURTEEN

IN HER MORE uncertain moments Stella had wondered whether all of the happiness of the last weeks had been an illusion, capable of disappearing in a puff of smoke. Maybe it had, because after three months of bliss, this last week had been excruciating. Horrible, uncertain…every other word that could be applied to a complete disaster.

Stella hadn't seen Rob; he'd been away at a medical conference to brush up on his networking and bring him up-to-date on some new developments in surgical techniques. That, at least, had taken the pressure off a bit.

Or loaded the pressure on, because this should be the one time when she really needed him. It *was* that time, even if Stella was struggling against the realisation.

She was due to drive down to Sussex on Saturday evening. By then the uncertainty of the situation was resolved. But she was still dealing with the fallout, with all of the solutions that had occurred to her, and mostly with the one that she knew she would have taken.

He was out in the garden, obviously unable to resist pulling up a few weeds that had appeared during the last week. Rob's face brightened when he saw her, and he pulled off his gardening gloves and enveloped her in a hug.

'I've really missed you.' She could feel his body against hers, and it was tempting to allow herself to just fall into that pleasure. Tell herself that everything was all right, and that there was no reason why they shouldn't resume their dangerous journey into the unknown.

'Are you okay? You look tired.' He knew immediately that something was bothering her.

'I haven't been sleeping.'

'Work?' He put his arm around her shoulders as they walked towards the back door and into the kitchen.

'No, I...' Stella sat down miserably. She'd spent most of drive convincing herself that she didn't need to tell Rob about something that might have happened but hadn't. But she'd been ducking the issue, because she knew exactly what her reaction would have been if it had.

He walked over to the kettle, making her a cup of tea and setting it down on the table, next to her elbow. Then he turned one of the kitchen chairs to face her and sat down.

'Come on. Spit it out.'

'It's nothing, Rob, really. My period started this morning.'

He nodded. That one piece of information told him everything, but it was impossible to gauge his reaction. Surprise, maybe. Concern, but that didn't say much because she couldn't divine what he was actually concerned about.

'How late were you?'

'A week. That doesn't sound like much, but I can normally set my watch by when my period arrives.'

'We've been careful.'

That had been her own first reaction. Disbelief. Counting through the number of times they'd been together and trying to work out where there might have been a slip.

'I know. Accidents happen and nothing's one hundred percent.'

'Not this time, though.' At least he wasn't laughing with relief. That was something.

'No, not this time.'

'You want to talk about it?' His fingers found hers and he squeezed her hand. This was all that she could want from a partner in these circumstances. He was concerned, and he seemed shaken by the news. But he was obviously waiting to find out how she felt and address that first.

'No.'

'Okay. Later, maybe…' Rob stood up, looking around the room, clearly trying to find something that urgently needed to be done. Then he sat back down again. 'You're sure?'

She needed to say this now. He wanted to hear how she felt and she wanted to tell him. She reached out to him, taking his hand.

'What is it you need to say to me, Stella? I can see something's bothering you and I'd like to know what it is.'

That was nice. Rob was being really nice about this, which was only making things worse. But she knew Rob well enough to wonder whether his own fears might kick in and he'd stop being quite so understanding when he found out what was on her mind. But she couldn't keep this from him, whatever the consequences.

'When I first thought I might be pregnant, I panicked. I kept telling myself that I couldn't be, but... I couldn't help thinking about the idea. What I might do, if I was...'

'Did you decide?' Rob was clearly trying to keep his composure, but she knew that fixed look on his face. He was struggling with something and when his hand went to his mouth it stayed there, as if to guard against words he might regret later.

'I decided that, whatever happened, if I was pregnant then I'd keep the baby. I really *wanted* the baby...'

Rob didn't hide the relief that showed in his face. Her first instinct was to kick him, for even thinking that she might have decided to end something so precious, but she could see where that was coming from. They'd never talked about it, and every woman weighed up that choice differently.

'You did a test?'

'Yes, I finally worked up the courage to do it

yesterday, and the kit said I wasn't pregnant. Then my period started this morning.'

'I'm so sorry, Stella. Even if you were never pregnant, you thought you were and that's a loss...' He shifted forward, putting his arms around her.

She could leave it at that. Accept that all of last week's worried uncertainty was over now. Understand that Rob's embrace, his care for her and everything they meant to one another *was* real. But that wasn't the point. It wasn't what had shaken her so badly.

'Rob, I... What would have happened? If I had been pregnant.'

'You wouldn't have done it on your own, if that's what's worrying you. I would have been with you all the way.'

That was what any woman faced with an unexpected pregnancy wanted to hear, wasn't it? It was what any woman wanted to hear full stop— that the man she loved wouldn't walk away when things got tough. She'd come to rely on Rob and to trust him, but Stella knew that he sometimes didn't trust himself.

'Does it frighten you, Rob?'

'Why should it?' He answered just a little too quickly. 'A baby's something special. The *most* special thing that could ever happen...'

'Someone who relies on you completely. I'd have to rely on you too.' Stella wasn't afraid of that, but she knew that Rob was. He still carried a lot of guilt over what he saw as letting others in his life down.

His face darkened. 'You're thinking that I can't step up and be a good father?'

'No, I'm not. I trust you, Rob. The question is whether you trust yourself.'

He couldn't answer that. Rob shook his head, clearly backing away from those thoughts.

'It doesn't matter now, Stella.' He spoke gently. 'You thought that you were pregnant, and that stirred up a lot of different feelings. I can understand that. But you aren't and we can move forward from that.'

Could they? Stella would have loved to be able to agree with him, to tell him that things between them could go on just as they had. But she'd got a glimpse of the future, and it was one that neither of them was ready for.

'It's not what either of us had planned, is it?' They hadn't planned anything. They'd lived for the day, knowing that their different lifestyles made it impossible for them to think ahead. But it had all worked too well, and Stella had fallen in love with him. Dared to dream that a future together might be a solution, when in fact it stood at the very heart of the problem.

'No. We could be more careful, maybe?'

'How? We've been careful, and we're both doctors so we both know pretty much everything there is to know about contraception. And that's not really the point. The point is that whatever we do together, we have to be able to take the consequences.'

He shook his head. 'There's always a solution, to any problem. It may not seem obvious at the time...'

'The solution *is* the problem, Rob.'

They'd somehow managed to put this aside, deciding to sleep on it and see how they felt in the morning. It was a relief when Stella agreed to his suggestion that they go out to eat, because having people around them was some kind of defence against blurting out the anger and the pain he was feeling.

Not with her. Never with her. At himself, because Stella had only told him the truth. The thought that she and a child might be dependent on him for their happiness was terrifying. He'd failed the people around him once, and if he failed Stella there would be no coming back from that.

Rob wondered whether she might choose to sleep in the spare room tonight, but she came with him to his bedroom. One last chance. A chance to show her how he felt about her, how much he loved her. But he left the light out as they undressed, and Stella didn't switch it on either. They were a pair of shadows who couldn't find each other in the darkness. When they slipped into opposite sides of the bed, the gulf between them was already too wide to cross. And each moment that he couldn't bring himself to touch her only made it wider.

Stella was right. The solution was the problem. They'd gone into this with their eyes wide open, they both knew what they were getting. Maybe, deep down, they'd both thought the same thing— that they'd spend a few delicious months together, pushing all the boundaries, and then they'd part as friends. But that had all gone horribly wrong when somehow, against all of the odds, their relationship had worked.

He lay awake for a long time, thinking it through and testing out all of the possibilities in his head. Stella was asleep, probably exhausted after a week of uncertainty, and it was comforting to know that at least saying what was on her mind had brought her some kind of respite. But when she stirred, whimpering in her sleep, he couldn't reach for her.

Rob rose early, showering and dressing before Stella was awake. Not knowing what else to do with himself, he went out into the garden, wandering amongst the fruit trees. That had always calmed him before, but this morning he could only see withered branches and decay all waiting to happen.

She joined him an hour later, bleary-eyed but trying to smile. Loving someone made it all too easy to put together the tiny clues that you'd otherwise miss, and something told Rob that Stella had woken up crying.

He had to put a stop to this. If he could bear his own pain, just to spend a few hours longer with her, then he couldn't bear hers. Rob ushered her back inside, switching the coffee machine on.

'I've been thinking about what you said yesterday. Do you still feel that way?' He put her coffee down in front of her and sat at the table.

Stella nodded, taking a sip of the strong brew. 'I have nothing to add, Rob.'

That was it, then, because he couldn't add anything either. He'd thought about it now and the prospect of being responsible for her happiness full-time terrified him. If they had to end, then he'd do it the best way he could. Rob took a deep breath, sucking in the air he'd need to survive this.

'You had the courage to say what we both knew all along. We always knew we weren't right for each other in the long-term, and it's time for us to accept that now. I just want to say that you'll always have a piece of my heart. I'll always be there for you, whenever you need a friend.'

A tear rolled down her cheek. 'I appreciate your honesty. I hope we can be friends too.'

'I couldn't have done what I have in the last few weeks without you. You came here and prised me out of my rut, and showed me that I could move forward again. You deserve every happiness that the future can give you and I have no regrets, Stella.'

Only that he'd caused her pain. That when she

left she was going to take the sunshine of the last few months with her. There was a growing list of the regrets that he'd never tell her about.

'Me neither. This is the right thing…isn't it?'

One last way back. A hint of uncertainty, a last chance. If he took it, it wouldn't change anything; it would just postpone this moment. Once was bad enough, and twice would be unbearable.

'Yeah. I'm sorry, but it is.'

She got to her feet, tearing a sheet from the roll of kitchen towel and blowing her nose on it, her movements suddenly brisk and businesslike. 'You're not going to do anything foolish, are you? Leave your job, I mean…'

Rob had been seriously thinking about it, but Stella's words made that impossible.

'That was one of the things we did together, and I don't want to throw it away. Unless you're uncomfortable with it?'

'No! We hardly see each other during the day, anyway.'

That wasn't entirely true, and maybe it was a hint that he should keep his distance. That was okay. If they both knew that was the score then it would be a lot easier. Rob could keep a low profile in the department and concentrate on his teaching; there was plenty for him to do there.

'And if we do happen to bump into each other, then we'll do what we've been doing all along. Just good friends, eh?'

'Friends. Yes, I'd like that.'

He'd like it too. He didn't see it happening for a while, because parting as friends carried with it the implication that they'd lost nothing. But it would be a workable Plan B, in case Plan A happened to fail and they found themselves thrown together.

Stella was looking at her watch. 'I should go...'

Not yet. He knew that this was coming, but he wanted just a few moments more. 'You'll stay and have some breakfast, surely. It's a long drive home.'

'I can stop for something on the way. If I get going before nine, then I'll miss most of the traffic at this end of the motorway.'

'Take some coffee at least.' Stella hesitated and he got to his feet. 'You can put the travel cup back in my pigeonhole if you want.'

'Yes. Thanks, some coffee would be nice.'

There were a few moments more, while Rob made the coffee and Stella went upstairs to gather her things. Then he walked her out to her car.

'Goodbye, Stella. Travel safe.' Today, and for the rest of your life. Be happy.

'You travel safe too.' She smiled up at him through the open car window, and he handed her the coffee. She stowed it in the cup holder, fiddling with the clip for a moment, and then drew the seat belt across her. Then it was time for him to step away.

Rob watched from the doorstep as the car started to make its way slowly along the lane and then disappeared amongst the hedgerows. Then he went inside, throwing himself down on the sofa in the sitting room. He felt like a man who had just arranged his own execution.

Sophie stirred from her usual sleeping place in front of the hearth, ambling over to nudge at his arm.

'What is it, Soph?' He spread his hands in the signal that Sophie had been taught to respond to, but she made no effort to point him in the direction of what she'd heard. Instead, she put her paws up onto his legs and nuzzled at his neck in an unusual display of exuberance.

Rob wondered if Sophie somehow knew that Stella had gone, and needed a bit of comfort too. He generally discouraged her from jumping up on the chairs, which wasn't difficult since Sophie had little interest in jumping anywhere these days, but Rob made an exception and lifted her up onto the cushions so that she could sprawl across his legs, leaning her head against his chest.

'Don't worry, Soph. I'm not going anywhere...'

He felt a tear roll down his cheek. Then another. It had been a very long time since he'd cried, and it felt strange. A release from the numb despair that he'd worked himself into three years ago. Stella had made him feel again—the good things and now the bad. This was her last gift to him.

# CHAPTER FIFTEEN

IT WAS ODD. Even though she'd thought that no one knew about her relationship with Rob, everyone seemed to know that it had ended. Stella had done her best to conceal the dark lines under her eyes, and she hadn't cried once at work, leaving that for when she got home. She supposed that it was more difficult to hide the fact that the sunshine that had been following her around recently had now quitted on her.

She hadn't seen Rob in the last two weeks. That was one thing she could be thankful for—that when he promised something he always found a way to deliver. She tried not to think about that too much either, because Rob's promises had always been so delicious.

Stella didn't want to go out, nor did she want to talk to anyone. But she'd told herself that life *did* go on, even if everything seemed to have stopped, and accepted her mother's invitation to Sunday lunch. Maybe the appearance of normality would help burnish the life she'd chosen for herself, because right now it seemed to have lost its shine.

'Darling!' Her father greeted her on the doorstep with a hug. 'We have some news for you.'

'Wait until she gets inside, Edward.' Her mother appeared behind him, wiping her hands on her apron. 'And I'll take a hug too...'

Hugging from two of her favourite people didn't help. Neither did the smell of Sunday lunch, which, if anything, was making Stella feel a little sick.

'What news, Dad?' Since it was highly unlikely that the news would have anything to do with Rob, it would at least take her mind off him for a while.

The usual flurry of organising drinks and deciding whether to sit outside or not ended up with white wine on the patio. Stella twisted the bottle in the ice bucket, inspecting the label.

'This isn't just for Sunday lunch, is it? Are Jamie and Chloe coming?' The wine was her father's favourite, very expensive, and reserved for big occasions.

'They were, but Jamie got a dose of norovirus and Chloe caught it. Then all the kids went down with it.'

That was no surprise. Jamie and his wife lived close to Chloe and her husband and the two families were in and out of each other's houses all the time. If her brother had caught something then it was pretty much a given thing that her sister would have got it, particularly something as easily transmittable as norovirus.

'Are they all right?'

'Yes, your father insisted on them all lining up so he could peer at them on the computer. He was going to go round there, but I told him that they'd already seen a doctor and they didn't need another one.'

'She's right, Dad.' Her father usually acted as if he was the only doctor in the world when his children and grandchildren were concerned. 'And it's the last thing you want to be taking into a hospital.'

'Yes, your mother went through all that. Although I am on holiday at the moment.'

'Really? Aren't you going to Norfolk in September as usual?' Something was clearly going on if her father was taking extra holidays. The thought occurred to Stella that he might be ill. 'Are you okay?'

'Never better. I've been doing some gardening.'

The garden *was* looking very tidy. Rob's fruit trees, and the therapeutic value of watching things grow, floated into her mind and Stella frowned. 'You're sure you're all right? And Mum?'

'You're going to have to tell her, Edward...'

'Tell me what?' Stella was on full alert now, and her father shot her a reproving glance.

'I'm in excellent health for my age, both physically and mentally, Stella. So is your mother; there's nothing for you to worry about in that respect.'

Right. That was a bit more like Dad; she could relax now. Maybe loss had put her on edge and she was overreacting.

'And we're buying a cottage. In Norfolk.' Her

mother clearly thought that her father was taking far too long to get around to The News.

'Oh. That's nice. You can go up there with Jamie or Chloe and spend some time with the kids, eh, Mum.'

'*We* can go up there. That's the plan. And of course you can come and join us all, whenever you like. Everyone needs a holiday from time to time. Remember how we all used to spend a month up there when you were little?'

Stella remembered. Days full of sunshine and sandy beaches. Her father would join them for two weeks, which had been the best two weeks of the year. A sudden yearning made her heart almost jump out of her chest, and she wiped a tear from her eye.

Her father was pouring the wine, and Stella resisted the temptation to stop him. Right now, she needed something that she could down in one gulp, and this wine commanded a bit more respect than that. She concentrated on the list of questions that had occurred to her, and asked the one that seemed the least controversial.

'How big is this cottage, Mum?'

Her father smiled, handing out the glasses and then pushing a manila envelope across the table to Stella. Inside was an estate agent's property portfolio, with pictures and floor plans.

'This is huge! And it's gorgeous…' Stella forgot all about respecting the contents of her glass and took a gulp of her wine. The house was a large gabled property, surrounded by wide lawns that led down to the sea. 'This must be five bedrooms at least.'

'Six. With en suite bathrooms.' Her father had always been a stickler for accuracy.

'You're not thinking of moving, are you?' Stella tried to remember if there was a large hospital within easy reach of the area that might attract a respected heart surgeon.

'No, not at the moment. I still have my work to consider.'

This all seemed very impractical. It was a lovely holiday home, but for just two weeks in the year, along with a few visits from Jamie and Chloe, it all seemed a bit over the top.

'I don't understand…'

'The thing is, Stella, I've been thinking a lot over the last couple of years.' Her father turned to her mother. 'We both have, haven't we, Margaret?'

Her mother nodded, smiling, leaving the explanations to her father.

'I spent a lot of time at work when you were little. I missed a very great deal and I regret that now.'

'We knew you were doing important work, Dad. And you were there for the big things.'

'I thought that was enough. But I realise that I should have been there for the little things as well.

I *wanted* to be there for the little things. It's too late for that now, but it's not too late to change. I have a wife who's put up with more than she should over the years, three wonderful children and four beautiful grandchildren. I want somewhere that they can all call home.'

'But…do Jamie and Chloe know about this?'

'Yes, it was actually their idea. They were talking about getting a place where both families could go for holidays and weekends, but when they looked into it they couldn't really afford it. Jamie showed me some of the estate agents' leaflets and said that it was going to be a longer-term plan than they'd bargained for. So I asked your mother to run away with me for a long weekend.'

All right. So Mum was in on this personality transplant idea as well.

Her mother was beaming now. 'We had a wonderful time, didn't we, Edward? It was right before Christmas and it was freezing, but we fell in love with the house as soon as we saw it. And your father went down on one knee and proposed on the spot.'

'Is there something you haven't been telling us, Mum?'

Her father chuckled, and her mother rolled her eyes. 'No, of course not. He was quite honest with me when he proposed the first time, and I knew exactly what I was getting. This time, he proposed a different kind of life, and I accepted.' Her mother held out her hand, displaying a new eternity ring on her finger, next to her wedding ring.

'That's gorgeous. Nice one, Dad.'

'We had a little ceremony on the beach, just the two of us. We made some new promises.' Her mother smiled.

'And then we had to go back to our hotel to warm up. I'm not sure whether it was horizontal hailstones or the sea was freezing.'

'It was beautiful, Edward. Just what I wanted.'

There had always been an understanding between her parents, and Stella had never doubted that they loved one another. But this was something new, a bright and different future for them both. Stella felt a tear roll down her cheek, and wiped it away.

'I'm so happy for you both. Truly. And you'll be working less from now on, Dad?'

'I've been in negotiations with the hospital, and we've agreed on thirteen days a month. That'll be enough to allow me to keep up with things, and to pass on my experience to the people who'll be taking over from me when I retire. That's only five years away now. And I hope you'll be able to join us for a few weekends when you have the time. Norfolk's only two hours away by train.'

'I will. I'm still learning though, Dad, you know that.'

'And things are changing from when I was a

medical student. I was at a conference only the other week, and I went to a session on work/life balance. There were a number of people there who had very different approaches to their work. One fellow had burned out three years ago, lost his marriage and had to leave his job...'

Stella froze. That would be far too much of a coincidence, although it would be the kind of session that would attract Rob. She didn't dare ask.

'... He spoke very well. Said that it had taken a while, but that he felt he'd recently found his future again, both personally and professionally. He said that he'd learned his lesson the hard way and that he felt that he should have...what was it... found his space.'

Breathe. Say *something*...

'That doesn't work for everyone, Dad. What was his specialty?' She could hardly ask for a name.

Her father shrugged. 'These things are all first names and no one's supposed to say where they come from or what they do. Some tomfoolery about anonymity, although I recognised quite a few faces there. And, frankly, if you can't put your name to your opinions...'

'Don't go on, Edward. No one's ever going to tell you that you're talking rubbish; you're far too senior. That's what I'm here for.'

'Yes, I suppose so. We have to think about the new generation of surgeons, who are still finding their feet.' Her father reached across, taking her mother's hand.

Rob had found his future. He'd said all of the right things to her and she hadn't listened, thinking that it was what he felt he had to say and not what he really wanted. It was just as well that her mother and father were so absorbed in each other, because Stella needed a bit of time to think this through.

'Stella? Darling, what's the matter?' She felt tears on her cheeks, and looked up to see her father staring at her.

'I just… I'm so…'

Her mother walked around the table and plopped herself down next to Stella, giving her a hug. One of those hugs that had been there all her life, whenever she'd skinned her knees or failed at something.

'We didn't mean to upset you, Stella. We just wanted to share this with you.'

'I know. And I'm just happy for you…'

Her father topped up her glass, but Stella ignored the wine and his worried face. 'You've always managed everything so well. But there's no shame in needing a break sometimes.'

Dad had always told her that, and Stella had listened. She'd made sure that she took enough time out, but that had just been because she knew she had to in order to keep working. Maybe she had to take a break for a different reason now.

'I'd love to come and see the house.'

'Of course.' Her mother gave her another hug. 'We signed the contract last week, and it's ours now.'

'Perhaps you'd like to choose your own room?' her father added. When they'd all gone on holiday together, she and Jamie and Chloe had taken it in turns to choose which bedroom they wanted.

'Thanks. I'd really like that.' Stella took the handkerchief that her mother proffered and dried her eyes. Now was the time for one of the biggest decisions of her life and suddenly she felt strong again.

'Mum and Dad. I'd like to propose a toast.' She picked up her glass and her parents followed suit. 'To new beginnings. Wherever we find them.'

Rob knew that things were serious when Phil asked him to the wine bar on Friday evening. Clearly this wasn't something that could be accomplished over an orange juice at lunchtime. When Phil spoke to the barman, indicating one of the bottles that was tucked away to one side, and bought two glasses of single malt Scotch, he knew that he was in for some straight talking.

Rob took a sip of the amber liquid, feeling its warmth at the back of his throat. Then he looked at his watch, in the vain hope that the last train down to Sussex might be leaving sooner than he'd thought.

'Let's find somewhere to sit down.' Phil made a beeline for one of the deep alcoves, each of which contained a table and several easy chairs. Putting his briefcase down on the table and taking off his jacket secured their claim to the booth, and Rob followed reluctantly. No hope that the din in the main bar might preclude any serious conversation, then.

'How are you doing, Rob? I know that you and Stella have broken up, and I haven't seen you around much.'

'It's better to make a clean break.' Rob gave in to the inevitable. 'I have plenty of other places to be, I don't need to loiter around making things awkward. How did you know?'

'Stella told me. You know how meticulous she is about everything, and I suppose she reckoned that having to notify me at the start of a relationship means that it's necessary to notify me at the end of it as well.'

Rob nodded. It was just the kind of thing that Stella would do, and a few weeks ago he'd have smiled at her insistence on order. Now it was just one more thing that he'd lost.

'So, I'll ask again. How are you doing, Rob?'

'I'm okay. We tried but it didn't work.' He took

a sip of his Scotch to wash the unpalatable truth from his lips.

'Okay like you were okay three years ago?'

Rob supposed he deserved that. He'd tried so hard to pretend that nothing was wrong three years ago and at the time he'd reckoned he was making a pretty good job of it. Looking back, it must have been obvious that something was going on.

'No. Really okay.'

Phil nodded. 'Because I haven't forgiven myself for going along with you the last time. I let you take some time off from surgery and concentrate on other things because I thought you just needed a break and that you were getting some help. I could have insisted on putting you on sick leave and I didn't.'

Enough. Rob's own guilt was bad enough, and Phil had been a good friend to him. He had nothing to reproach himself for.

'How long do you suppose it would have taken me to get certified fit for work again? I'm a doctor, I know exactly what to say to get myself signed off. And I told you that I was getting help when I wasn't. That's not your fault; it's mine.'

'I suppose there is that to it.' Phil leaned back in his seat. 'But you understand why *okay* isn't really cutting it with me.'

Yes, and it was a challenge. What could he say to make a friend believe him, when he was saying exactly the same things as he had three years ago? He'd been lying then—why not now?

'Rob...?' Phil had left him to think about it, but he wanted an answer.

'Because I loved her. The things she's marvellous at, and those she's not so great at. Everything in between, including the idiosyncrasies and the things that make you wonder if she's on the same planet as you are.'

Phil looked at him blankly. Clearly, he'd never considered Stella to be on a different planet from anyone else, but she tended not to emphasise the impish side of her nature when she was at work.

'Don't ever tell her I said that, will you.'

'My lips are sealed. Go on, Rob.'

Now that he'd started, it was easier to finish. 'I'm feeling a lot of grief over losing Stella. But that's a real thing, a normal reaction to something that's happened to me. You know as well as I do that clinical depression and anxiety don't work that way, they're medical conditions. I loved her, and I could feel that love. I lost her, and I'm feeling that too, but it's not the same as three years ago. I'm okay, really.'

Phil nodded. 'I get that. I'm sorry to hear it, though.'

'Thanks. And I appreciate your asking.'

They sat in silence for a while, savouring their drinks. Then Phil looked at his watch, prompting Rob to look at his.

'My train...'

Phil smiled. 'Yes. Mine too. If I catch this one, I'll be home in time for supper.'

They were heading in different directions, and outside the wine bar Rob stopped, shaking Phil's hand.

'Good talk.'

Phil looked a little mystified. 'I'm glad it helped. I'll see you next week.'

It had been an excellent talk, and Rob's mind was buzzing as he walked to the station. *Real.* What he'd had with Stella was real. He could feel it still, powering him forward. He'd loved Stella and he'd lost her, and now he could do something about that.

# CHAPTER SIXTEEN

MONDAY HAD BEEN a better day. Not a great day, but a better one, because Stella had begun to feel that she had choices ahead of her, instead of the one path that she'd followed all of her working life. Maybe by Thursday she would have worked up the courage to ask Rob if he'd go for coffee with her.

Thursday was a long way away, and Monday seemed to be keeping hold of her much longer than it should. She arrived home at eight in the evening, wondering if it was too early to go straight to bed.

And then she saw him. Sitting on the steps outside her block, his elbows propped on his knees, looking up and down the road and… Rob had seen her now. He got to his feet, waiting for her.

Too soon. She hadn't worked out what she wanted to say to him yet. Maybe she should send him away, and tell him that she'd meet up with him for coffee on Thursday. But he'd clearly made this unscheduled journey up to London for some reason. Her treacherous hopes were whispering in her ear that maybe Rob had come to see her, and it was impossible to slow her footsteps back to a normal pace as she hurried towards him.

She stopped in front of him, trying not to stare.

If he'd come to see her, then presumably he'd worked out something to say, to break the awkward silence.

'I came to talk, Stella. Will you hear me out?'

'Yes.' She hurried up the steps, knowing that he was right behind her. Dropped her keys, and he picked them up, putting them back into her hand without allowing his fingers to touch hers. Good. That was good. If he touched her now, and she had to let him go...

The lift wasn't working, and she made for the stairs, powering herself up them. He was still behind her when she reached her front door and let him in, wondering if everything was as tidy as it should be, and dismissing the thought. Her flat was generally more orderly than Rob's house, where things seemed to move around and get lost of their own accord, and anyway she doubted he'd come to inspect her housekeeping.

She turned to him, still slightly breathless from the stairs. 'Would you like some tea?'

'That would be nice. Thank you.'

So well mannered. They'd never been this polite to each other, even when they'd first met, and right now Stella wanted to engage in something very different with him. Punish him for hurting her, maybe, or just forget about all of that and engage in a little bad-mannered sex.

She dropped her handbag onto the floor and hung her jacket up, draping it carelessly over the hook so that it was left dangling by one sleeve. Rob followed her into the kitchen and she motioned for him to sit down while she made the drinks, throwing the teabags into the cups with unnecessary force. Even though her back was turned, she was aware that he was watching her.

Finally, she could go and sit down at the table, pushing his cup towards him. Now it was all up to Rob.

He reached into his jacket pocket, taking something out, and dropping a small box onto the table between them. A ring box, with the name of one of London's best jewellers in gold on the top.

'What's that, Rob?' She wrapped her hands around her cup, to stop them from inching towards the box.

'You know what it is. And it's non-negotiable. It's the one thing I'm not going to compromise on.'

'Do I have a say in the matter?'

'You always have a say in everything. But it's only fair to let you know where I stand, and that I can't stop loving you, Stella.'

She puffed out a breath. This was the big league. But she was used to high stakes, and she could deal with them. 'What *is* negotiable, Rob?'

'Everything else. I let you go because I was afraid. I've let a lot of people down, and I couldn't trust that I'd changed enough not to let you down. But I'd missed one very important thing. What we had was real. I can't let you down, because it won't allow me to.'

This. Just this was all she wanted. 'I can't stop loving you, Rob. However inconvenient it is.'

He laughed suddenly. 'I'm an inconvenience, am I?'

'No! But I think we both have to admit that we've got very different lives. Please tell me you have a plan…'

'No plan. What we have right now is good enough for the time being. We can spend Thursdays and Fridays together in London, and Saturdays and Sundays in Sussex. We can work from there for a more long-term solution. I could give up my job and come to London.'

'And give up your beautiful house? I won't have that, Rob. It's so much a part of you. Sussex does have hospitals, and hospitals have surgeons.'

'We'll see. There's clearly still some negotiating to do there.' His gaze caught hers, and Stella knew that the most important question was still to come. 'Whether or not we have children—that's got to be your decision. If you decide that you want to be a mother, then maybe I'll get to step up to the ultimate challenge of being a stay-at-home dad.'

'I get to do my share too. You think I'm going to miss out on first steps and scraped knees? Giving them a hug at bedtime and telling them a story…' The look on Rob's face said it all. He wanted a

family as much as she did. 'There's some negotiating to do there as well, I suppose.'

'Clearly. I'll share the scraped knees with you,
if you share the dirty nappies with me. We'll work
it out.'

Stella reached for him, grasping his hands tightly
in hers. 'Can we do this, Rob? Can we really do it?'

'We can do it. Just say the word, Stella.' He
grinned suddenly. 'On second thoughts, I'm going
to say the word…'

He reached for the box, but Stella got there first,
opening the lid. Inside, a ring with five sparkling
diamonds in a bezel setting, the thin platinum rim
snaking elegantly around each stone to protect the
sides from snagging.

'Rob, it's beautiful.'

He took the ring from the box, falling to one
knee in front of her. Stella was trembling with excitement, hardly able to sit still.

'I can't promise you everything, Stella, but together we can do anything. Will you marry me?'

'Yes, Rob. I love you so much, and I can't wait
to find out what that anything is.'

He took her hand, putting the ring onto her finger. Stella flung her arms around his neck, kissing him.

'Can you stay?'

'Yes, I have tomorrow and Wednesday off work.
I reckoned that I'd need a couple of days to plot
my next move if you sent me away.'

'I couldn't have done that. You're stuck with me now, whatever happens. If things get tough, then we'll work them out together.' Maybe Rob needed to hear that.

'I know. But I love you for saying it.' He kissed her again. 'How do you want to take this, Stella?'

'For starters? I can't work out what I want to do first. Talk and make plans with you or make love…'

'What do you say to going out to eat first, and then we'll have all night to make love? If we're together then the plans will grow on their own.'

'That sounds marvellous. Just beautiful.'

# EPILOGUE

*Two years later*

TODAY WAS A big day. A marquee had been erected outside, and the house was looking its best. All the food was laid out in the kitchen, waiting to be carried outside when the time came. And they were late.

'Did the alarm go off?' Stella sat up in bed, rubbing her eyes.

'Uh? I think it must have done. Why don't you shower first…?'

'What, so you can spend an extra five minutes in bed?'

'Nope. I need a serious man-to-man talk before we leave…' He got out of bed, walking over to the crib to pick Daniel up.

It never got old. Seeing her gorgeous husband and their beautiful six-month-old son together. Rob cradled the baby in his arms and Daniel's blue-grey eyes focused on his father's face, his hands reaching towards him.

'I'll shower and get dressed then. You can go through what Daniel needs to do today with him.'

'Will do…' Rob grinned at her and as she got

out of bed she heard him talking to Daniel. 'It's pretty easy really. These old churches really echo, and you'll be surprised at how far your voice will carry. When we give you to Phil to hold, just take a deep breath and give it all you've got.'

'Don't underestimate Phil. Liz told me he was the family baby whisperer when their girls were small.' Stella made for the shower, chuckling at the secret Phil's wife had shared with her.

'Babies are supposed to cry at christenings, aren't they?' Rob called after her.

'He'll do whatever he decides to do, you can't organise that,' Stella shot back at him.

They'd made many plans in the last two years. Several of them had come to nothing. Stella's idea that they might go into general practice together barely saw the sun go down on it, and Rob's idea that they could move to London, and he would take on the renovation of a new house there, shrivelled and died over one idyllic weekend at the Sussex house that they both loved so much.

In the end, the opportunities had presented themselves. Stella's pregnancy had coincided with a job offer to head up the small Reconstructive Surgery unit at a Sussex hospital. The construction of a new hospital on the site was already underway, and her new employers were taking a long-term approach to developing the unit. They'd been open to Stella starting work after the baby was born, and she had already begun the challenge of developing the existing unit in preparation for creating a centre of excellence in the state-of-the-art operating suites that the new building would provide.

Rob spent one day a week in surgery up in London, and the rest of his time was spent on teaching and research. His unconventional approach to both of those tasks gave him a lot of freedom, and much of the preparatory work was done in the butterfly filled conservatory that now contained two desks.

Daniel had his father's eyes and his mother's determination, and he had captained the process of change. He had high standards and many demands, but fulfilling them was the most rewarding task that Stella and Rob had taken on together. Both his mother and father were hands-on parents, and Stella's mum and dad leapt at the chance of caring for their grandson for one day a week. Her father was catching up on what he'd missed when his own children were babies, and Stella loved watching him with Daniel almost as much as her mother did.

It was a busy life, which required organisation and out of the box thinking. But their family times and time for just the two of them were all built into the plan, the bedrock of everything else that they did.

They were almost ready now. Stella was brushing her hair, fixing it up at the back of her head in the soft style that Rob always said he liked so much, trying to think of anything they might have forgotten.

'Christening shawl?' They couldn't turn up without the lacy white shawl that Rob had been christened in and his parents had lent them.

'Done. It's a bit warm for him outside the church, so I've put it in the baby bag and we can take it out as soon as we see my mum on the horizon.'

'Good thought. Order of service?'

'Two copies in your handbag.' Rob grinned. 'Done.'

'Um… Guests?'

'They'll sort themselves out. We've got more than enough food, and a marquee in case it rains.' Rob looked out of the window, checking that the marquee hadn't disappeared during the night.

'That's it, then.' She turned, looking at Rob. 'Your shoes?'

'They're somewhere…' Rob put Daniel down, brushing at the damp patch on the shoulder of his shirt. 'Ah. Got them. Done.'

They tumbled out of the house, taking the footpath that led down to the village. Daniel's christening was an informal affair, most of the guests abandoning their cars on the outskirts of the village and walking the rest of the way to the church in a nod to one of the older traditions of the village.

Stella's parents were waiting for them where the footpath wound around the back of the station, chatting in the sunshine with Rob's two sisters.

There was a brief, friendly tug-of-war between Rob and her father, before Rob gave in gracefully, giving Daniel to his grandfather to carry.

When they strolled together along the path to the church they could see Rob's parents approaching from the other direction, the rest of their combined families already waiting in the sunny churchyard. People from the village were appearing from various directions, coming just as they were to welcome little Daniel into their community. Phil and Liz Chamberlain were chatting to Emma, who seemed to be pointing out the main architectural features of the old church.

'Could this be any more perfect?' Rob murmured. Stella glanced towards the crowd of their family and friends and smiled up at him.

'I'm struggling to think how today could have turned out any better.'

'Me too. Only I've given up the struggling part. The funny part of accepting that you can't have everything...'

'Is that suddenly you find you have all that you want?' Stella smiled up at him. They'd discovered that truth in the very early days of their marriage.

He stopped walking, putting his arms around her shoulders and brushing a kiss against her lips. Today was turning out to be everything that Stella had wanted it to be.

'First day of the rest of our lives.' Rob had said that to her on their wedding day, and at the start of many other days since. 'What do you suppose this one's going to bring?'

The same happiness that had shaped all the others.

'Wait and see, Rob. Let's just wait and see.'

* * * * *

*If you enjoyed this story, check out these other great reads from Annie Claydon*

Healed by Her Rival Doc
One Summer in Sydney
Children's Doc to Heal Her Heart
Cinderella in the Surgeon's Castle

*All available now!*